ADRIAN'S
WAR

LLOYD TACKITT

First Edition: August 2012

ISBN: 1478297700
ISBN-13: 978-1478297703

Editor: Everything Indie, www.everything-indie.com.
Cover Design: Streetlight Graphics, www.streetlightgraphics.com

DEDICATION

This book is dedicated to my father, William Nathan Tackitt. He is a veteran of three wars; WWII, Korea, and Vietnam. A quiet man with immense dignity and modesty. A true life hero, and gentleman, in every sense of the words.

FOREWORD

AS IN THE FIRST NOVEL in this series "A Distant Eden" this is a hybrid between how-to and fiction. It contains information on survival techniques for primitive survival situations. Techniques that are useful when you have nothing man-made at hand to work with. They are not described in detail, but are easy to research on the internet. Those techniques are found primarily in the first half of the book.

The second half of the book contains information on fighting raiders, based on classic guerrilla tactics. In a post-apocalyptic world raiders will be a fact of life. Historically they have nearly always been a fact of life from the time agriculture was developed. Every survival situation will have its own unique set of circumstances; they won't be identical to the story you read here. The specific methods you would have to use may be different given your situation, but the overall guerilla style of resistance is the same. You will gain insight into how to resist if necessary.

The fictional story line is intended to show how, when, and where the techniques could be applied. It has been demonstrated that learning from an entertaining story line is better retained in memory. This is reinforced by the additional effort of doing one's own research. The internet makes that research easy. Combined, the story with research, your chances of being mentally prepared are improved significantly.

PRELUDE

Winter, 2015

ADRIAN THRUST THE SPEAR INTO the bear's open mouth, cutting its tongue badly. The bear roared and flung its head from side to side at the stinging pain, then charged again, furiously snapping its jaws like huge steel traps, and swinging at him with long, sharp claws. Adrian backed up carefully, ducking and dodging, continually stabbing the spear at the bear's nose and face.

He had been startled to find a grizzly bear in these mountains this time of year; most bears were in hibernation. The bear had looked at Adrian as though he were food, and Adrian had instantly seen the bear as a life or death challenge. They both refused to back down from this fight to the death. Almost on first sight, they charged at each other. Adrian was armed with a flint-tipped spear. It was a tiny weapon against the two thousand pound bear, but Adrian wasn't concerned with losing. If he lost, he lost. That was all there was to it. He'd had no intention of losing, but was well aware that he could.

Adrian felt the back of his thighs press against a large fallen log. He was pinned. He couldn't back up any farther without taking the time to climb over the log, and that would be all the opening the bear needed to finish Adrian off.

Late Summer, 2014

Alice said, "Happy anniversary Adrian!"

"Happy anniversary to you, baby. It's been a great year, the best in my entire life. But I bet it's not as good as next year. Hey, I have a present for you."

Adrian went outside and returned after a moment carrying a basket. As he handed it to her, he said, "Made this for you. Worked on it whenever you were at the hospital so it'd be a surprise."

"It's gorgeous! You made this? Where in the world did you learn to make such intricate patterns?" Alice said, looking it over admiringly.

In the hospital recovering from a car wreck when I was a kid. They had a basket weaving class. They told me I was a natural."

"It's fantastic! She gave him a kiss. I made you something too. Worked on it in when we didn't have patients." Alice disappeared into the bedroom and rummaged in the back of a closet. She emerged with a wrapped package. Adrian unwrapped it and held up a pair of moccasin boots made from soft pigskin.

"Too cool! I love these! Well made, and they look good, too." Adrian untied his hiking boots and removed them, then pulled on the new boots; their tops came nearly to his knees. "Perfect fit." He walked around the living room in them. "Feels great! Just the ticket for hunting. I'll be able to feel small twigs under my feet before stepping down and making a noise. They'll be great for running too. Wonderful."

Adrian playfully walked up to Alice as though he was stalking a deer, then gave her a big hug and a long kiss. "Thanks baby. These are great. I'll break them in today when I go hunting."

"I have to leave for the hospital or I'll be late relieving Rebecca. But I have one more present for you." She dug into her pocket and handed Adrian a harmonica. "Sarah told me that you used to play when you were a kid. She said you were a fantastic player, had a natural gift. It used to break her heart, hearing you play late at night when you were sad, but she hasn't heard you play in years. I set a broken arm in exchange for this. I would love to hear you play sometime, so practice up. Love you, gotta go."

Adrian leaned in the door opening, his six-foot four-inch frame nearly filling it, and watched Alice walk towards the field hospital, the old familiar feel of the harmonica in his hand. He hadn't played in years, not since going into the army, but he knew he wouldn't need much practice.

As he admired her form, and the sensual way she moved, he thought, "She even walks with a southern accent." He reflected on the past year. It had been a good year, all things considered. It was preceded, however, by a ghastly year; after a coronal mass ejection larger than the Carrington event had destroyed the world's power grids.

First and second world countries had become too dependent on a lifestyle powered by a complicated electrical grid system that was vulnerable to large solar ejections. This weakness had been known for years; congressional hearings had been held to discuss the matter, but almost nothing was done to harden the grid against this known threat. Instead, the operators intended to rely on having enough advance warning to shut down and disconnect the massive transformers. But the CME that knocked the grid out two years previously came too swiftly for that to happen. Most of the huge transformers blew up, transformers that at best would take three years to replace. But with no electric power to make more of them, they proved to be irreplaceable. It was a chicken and egg problem: transformers were needed to supply power to make transformers. There was no power. The grid was down, permanently.

When the power went off, the pumping of water and fuel stopped. Riots quickly broke out in the streets when people realized that there would never again be food delivered to the grocery stores. Within weeks, the old and very young and those dependent on modern medicines had died. Starving people by the millions left the cities in search of food in the countryside. Mass starvation took hold as the scarce resources in rural areas were overwhelmed by the sheer numbers of urban emigrants, and their meager food stores were rapidly depleted. Small and large game were either killed or fled in front of the waves of the walking starved. Livestock hadn't stood a chance.

Each city rapidly became surrounded by miles of country devoid of any living thing, including edible insects. Human bodies were scattered everywhere. The magnetic storm came in December, and people in the north died by the millions from exposure to the cold before they could starve. For months the stench of human decay filled the air, even miles away from the multitude of bodies. Cannibalism became rampant. It took a year for the population to stabilize at three percent of what it had been before the CME. Only around 18 million people inhabited America. Suicide, especially murder-suicides involving entire families, had become common as millions decided quick death was preferable to inevitable starvation and watching loved ones die day-by-day. It was a horrendous ending, but one often selected as better than the alternatives.

Adrian's uncle, Roman, was a prepper before the solar storm. He had built his home in a remote location an hour and a half commute south of Fort Worth, on the bank of the Brazos River. There he stockpiled food supplies; antique tools, survival books, and anything else that he thought might someday be of use. Adrian and five of his platoon mates had been provisionally discharged from the army, along with most of the armed forces, because the military could no longer feed them. He and his buddies had walked to Roman's home and joined up with Roman, Sarah, and their children and grandchildren. There they had started to rebuild a life of sorts by hunting, fishing, and eventually farming.

Along the way, Adrian had stopped at a hospital in Waco to gather medical tools and equipment that might be useful. There he found Alice, along with another doctor and six nurses, hiding on the upper floor. They were near starvation and asked to be taken along. At first Adrian had refused, but Alice strenuously explained that she and the other women were trained medical professionals with valuable skills. Adrian, admiring her spirit and her logic, relented. He knew it was one of the best decisions he had ever made.

Shortly after arriving at Roman's, a hostile survival group had discovered Adrian and his companions. They would have taken them as slave laborers, to be worked to death. Adrian assembled a combat operation that wiped out the threat before it could fulminate. They stabilized the area and created a system of trade with others in the area. Alice and her team set up a field hospital that quickly became a magnet for anyone in the area needing medical help. This became the center of civilization for many miles around, and Roman's small, ragtag family quickly grew into a village locally known as Fort Brazos.

With time, a lot of hard, backbreaking work and no shortage of luck, they established small farms and key "industries": a blacksmith, a cobbler, a distillery, a trading post, tobacco operations, candle making, and a tannery. Matthew, the community's blacksmith and preacher, had perfected a portable wood gas generator that could run power generators and most gasoline or natural gas-fueled internal combustion engines. The hospital utilized more electrical power than any of the industries, and had several generators ready to be fired up as needed. Matthew adapted tractors and trucks to run on wood gas by mounting the gas generators directly onto them. The trucks could cover long distances and haul loads, stopping occasionally to put more wood into the burner. They were useful for going into the deserted cities on scavenging trips. Tractors were run the same way, allowing increased farm productivity to the point that they were now generating a modest surplus of food to use in trade.

Adrian and his former army buddies dabbled a bit at farming, keeping small plots going for their own use, but their primary responsibilities were security and hunting. They were all trained and efficient former special operations soldiers. They had been selected by the military for the specialized assignments in part because they had no immediate families. They routinely scouted in wide circles around their extended area, traveling for days and sometimes weeks at a time, looking for security threats, meeting and mixing with other small villages and tribes; spreading the word about the hospital and trading post. These trips were combined with hunting when they were returning, bringing in much needed and welcomed meat. Livestock rearing at Fort Brazos was an ongoing process, but it takes time to build herds. It would take a few more years before harvesting a surplus could happen.

When Alice was out of sight, Adrian retrieved his rifle and walked into the woods still wearing his new moccasin boots. He wasn't going far today; hunting was on the agenda, not scouting. Deer were scarce. There hadn't been large populations of them in the area before the grid went down, and the ones that had been there were nearly wiped out or else had fled. It would take years before their population fully recovered. Feral hogs, on the other hand, were abundant. The hog population in Texas before the CME had been huge, and almost doubled on an annual basis. They too had taken a population hit, but not nearly as extreme as the deer because hogs were equipped to fight back against encroachment.

Deer will only produce up to two fawns per year, but hogs could produce as many as twenty, and those twenty would be breeding within their first year of life. Within the first year after the collapse the hogs had already recovered their previous numbers and were rapidly expanding again. They out-competed deer for food, further restraining the deer population's recovery. As Roman put it, "The hogs are to us what the buffalo were to the plains Indians." And it was true. The survival of Fort Brazos had been largely dependent on the growing hog population.

Hogs, like all animals, are creatures of habit. Adrian had long learned their habits and knew where and when to look for them. Hogs were easier to hunt than deer, which ran at the first inkling of danger. Hogs often turned and attacked instead. Hogs were smart, vicious, and deadly fighters, but they had little chance against a skilled shooter.

Roman had abandoned his home on the riverbank because the river was no longer flood controlled. The upstream dam gates would never work again and soon the river would be wild and prone to periodic flooding. He knew his home would be underwater at some point. He had moved to a farmstead that had been constructed in the late 1800's. The most recent owners had been killed by looters soon after the grid dropped. The farm was originally built when Indian attacks were a threat; the buildings were arranged to be easily defended, made of thick, bullet-stopping cedar logs. It was not far from the flood line of the river below, making fresh water easily accessible.

Adrian brought home a large hog that evening, dragging it on a quickly made travois. By the time Alice came home from her shift at the hospital, he had butchered the hog and taken it into the smoke house where it would hang for several weeks being smoke cured. While he was cutting up the hog, a task he had performed so many times that he no longer had to think about it, he reminisced about their year together. He recalled a conversation he and Alice had when he proposed marriage a year ago.

"I love you Adrian, but I'm not sure about marriage," Alice had said. "There's something I can't shake. My father killed himself when I was twelve. He blew his head off with a shotgun. I heard the explosion and ran to see what it was, and found his body. It was gruesome. I went into shock, totally catatonic for two months. I still have horrible nightmares."

Adrian interrupted. "I am so sorry baby."

Alice barely noticing the interruption continued. "Suicide is obscene, the ultimate obscenity of all obscenities. Killing yourself where your daughter will find you is the ultimate rejection. I know that I was not the cause; he was mentally ill...but there is a feeling I... fear—no, it's closer to terror. I'm afraid to commit to anyone that could do that to me again. It terrifies me that if I give my heart I might..." Alice made a soft choking sound and looked down.

Adrian held her close and said softly, "I've never had a suicidal thought in my life. I had a friend that killed himself. I'm still pissed. It's a cheap way to treat your friends. I would have done anything in the world to help him, but he just went off and killed himself. I'll never forgive him for that. I can't imagine what you went through, a million times worse, at least."

Alice said. "It's a nightmare."

Adrian replied. "What do you need to hear from me, or know about me, that will make you believe I won't do that? How can I prove that? The only thing I can do is swear I will never kill myself, no matter what, no matter how bad it gets."

Adrian knew that her concern was valid; she wasn't

being melodramatic. Suicide wasn't an isolated event these days. Many millions had killed themselves since the grid went down. Many still took that way out rather than face the hardships of survival. It was a common occurrence.

Alice gripped his hand. "Promise you'll never consider it. Never."

"I swear it. I swear it from my heart. Never, under any circumstance, for any reason."

Alice still had the nightmares, but over their year of marriage they had come less often and were less vivid. Adrian didn't know it at the time, but that sworn declaration would play a key role in keeping him alive, or he might well have taken that way out himself.

Spring 2015

Over time the Fort Brazos field hospital had drawn people from hundreds of miles. This was good for the village, but became a curse for Adrian. Alice worked long days and nights with only occasional days off. The flow of patients was far from steady. They would come in waves, followed by long periods of no one at all. She bore the brunt of the work because she loved healing. To her, practicing medicine wasn't about her need to serve, it was about the sick and injured. It was about using every skill and talent she had to heal. She was a much of a warrior as her husband, with a different outcome when successful. They made an odd match, the healer and the killer, but it was a match that worked. They were well-suited in temperament and intellect.

It was Alice's diligence that killed her. It started on a

slow day of a slow week. There were no patients in the hospital, and Alice had sent the entire staff home. She was inventorying their sparse medicinal supplies when a man knocked on the open door and asked for help. He had running sores on his face and arms. Alice took a long look at him, then led him to the nearest room and told him to lie down. She said she'd be right back.

Alice went outside, spotted Matthew nearby, and shouted to him. "Matthew, come here please." Matthew immediately turned and headed toward her. When he was fifty feet away she shouted, "Stop Right There! Don't come any closer. I have a patient that may be contagious."

Matthew stopped, alarmed.

"I need you to spread the word to everyone to stay far away from the hospital until I can confirm the diagnosis" Alice continued. "Otherwise it could wipe out the village. Make sure you tell Adrian to stay away. He'll want to come, but I am already exposed and there is no going back. I absolutely forbid him to come near. Tell him in those words; make him understand he is under strict orders from me to stay away. He can wait by that tree over there, no closer, and when I know something I'll come out and tell him. Please, will you do that?"

The patient died the next day. Alice wouldn't let anyone near the hospital until she determined if she herself was infected. By the fourth day, she knew she was. She called out to Adrian, who had come to wait by the nearby tree, just as she had expected. "Bring me a weeks' worth of food and water, leave it halfway between us, and then walk back. I'll stay here and see if I can pull myself through this. Now, listen to me. If you try to come in here I have a syringe already loaded with an overdose of barbiturates. I swear to God I will use it on myself before you get halfway to the door. I'm infected and I can deal with that. I've always known this could happen; it's a condition of my profession, one we all accept as physicians. But if you get infected...I...I couldn't deal with that. You know how I feel about this, so please...don't make me do it.

"If I die, burn this building to the ground. It's the only way to be sure the infection doesn't spread. Burn it with me inside, but don't enter; burn it from the outside, and stay on the up-wind side. Keep the generators running all the time until then. I want that body to stay cold. Make sure the building burns hot and that my body, and his, are completely incinerated." Alice sobbed and turned back into the building, closing the door behind her.

Adrian stood guard at the point Alice had told him not to cross. He camped out on the spot, leaving only occasionally for sanitary breaks. Sarah brought him meals three times a day. Alice and Adrian talked frequently as best they could across the distance they had to maintain. The entire village stayed away and out of sight, giving them what little privacy they could have, and avoiding the plague inside. As Alice weakened, their conversations grew less frequent.

Alice died after ten days. She had grown too weak to stand without supporting herself against the doorframe. She couldn't shout loud enough for Adrian to hear her anymore, but he could see her well enough to know she was covered with pustules. His heart was beyond breaking; it was shattered. She had come to the door several times every day to speak to him, then it became only two times per day, and then one. Then, on the ninth day, she didn't appear. He knew she was gone. He waited three more days before he completely gave up. Honoring her last wish that he keep his distance, had been the hardest thing he had ever done in his life, and he knew nothing would ever come close to being so difficult. But honoring her request was the last and best thing he could do for her. The smell of decomposing flesh wafted out to him as he approached the building with a bucket of hot lard mixed with some carefully hoarded diesel fuel. He alone approached the building; it was his wife, his duty.

The building burned for two days, and it was another two days before the ashes had cooled enough that he could search for her remains. It had been a long, hot fire, but he expected to find some of her bones. He knew which bed she had used, so he knew where to start looking. He found her remains, and knelt in the ashes silently. He carefully brushed the ashes from around her scorched bones; much like an archaeologist would, and began gently placing them in a quilt-lined box that Sarah had prepared. He would place her remains into a full size coffin and she would be given a funeral service and burial, then he would leave for the mountains in Colorado. As he collected the bones, he wept. Her skull was especially difficult for him.

Her remains were partially covered by a piece of sheetrock and fiberglass insulation that had fallen from the ceiling during the fire, protecting her stomach area from some of the heat. With utter disbelief he found a tiny partial skull nestled in her pelvis. It was comprised of cartilage and had been darkened and hardened by the heat, but had been somewhat protected by the sheetrock and insulation. Its shape was unmistakable. Alice had been pregnant, and he hadn't known. Shock coursed through his body as he realized what he was holding. He was stunned and unable to move for a long time. Gathering his will, he carefully collected every bone and piece of cartilage he could find and placed them in the box, then returned home where he tenderly laid them in the coffin that waited there. He walked to Roman and Sarah's house after washing the ashes from his body and changing clothes.

The horror on his face told Sarah what he had discovered. "Oh God, I wish you hadn't found out," she said. "She was so thrilled to be carrying your child. She was waiting until she was absolutely sure, one hundred percent sure, before she would tell you. She didn't want to be wrong and get your hopes up. She made me promise not to tell you, and then when she got sick and you didn't know, I...I couldn't tell you. I wouldn't have anyway; a promise to Alice was a promise kept and it would have been so much better if you didn't know."

CHAPTER 1

ADRIAN HAD KILLED MORE THAN his share of men in his life, yet this was his first funeral. He had missed his parent's double funeral; he was in the hospital recovering at the time. He felt betrayed by the weather; it should have been a cold, gray, rainy day, wintry and exemplifying death. Instead it was a sunny, late spring morning bursting with the promise of new life. Adrian hated everything about it. He and Alice had been married for only eighteen happy months.

Roman put his hand gently on Adrian's shoulder. They stood silently for a few moments, staring down at the freshly turned earth.

Roman said, "I wish there were words that would ease the pain, even just a little. But there aren't. Words won't heal this." Roman dropped his hand from Adrian's shoulder, gently grasping his elbow instead. With light pressure he turned Adrian to face him.

"I know you've heard time heals all, and you probably don't believe it right now...but it's true. Time passes, and with it the pain eases and someday you'll find you're able to move on. Before that, though, the pain is going to get deeper and harder to bear. A lot worse."

Roman released his elbow. Holding eye contact, he continued. "You're still in shock. You're in the early stages. I hate to say this, but you should know. It'll take months before the pain bottoms out, before you reach the lowest point. You'll remain there for what will seem like eternity. But eventually, gradually, the pain will lessen a tiny bit with each passing day. It'll never be gone. It will always be right there behind your eyes. But you'll reach the point where you carry on, day to day, without it being the only thing in your mind."

Roman dropped his eyes back to the grave, the sweet smell of fresh turned earth filling his lungs. He stared at the simple grave marker without really seeing it. It was quiet, the only sounds the singing of a mockingbird, a slight rustling of leaves from the soft breeze.

Adrian looked back to the grave. He didn't want to hear Roman's empty words. He was barely paying attention, oblivious to the smells and sounds surrounding him, oblivious to everything except what Roman's insistence forced him to confront. Only deep love and respect for his uncle kept him from turning his back on him.

Roman looked back up at Adrian, sorrow evident in the set of his shoulders and the look on his face. "You need to know what will happen. You shouldn't have to learn this in hind-sight. You'll have peace with this someday. I want you to know that. "

Roman stepped closer, aware of Adrian's emotional distance, trying to close the gulf physically. "I'll say this and leave you alone. Sarah and I don't want you to go to the mountains now. We want you to stay here, with family and friends. Being alone right probably now seems like the best thing in the world, but it's not. You should be around the people who love you, long enough to start healing. Wait a while. Stay here with us."

Roman moved back to Sarah. He knew Adrian was not convinced; he could tell by the tension in Adrian's neck and the tightness of his jaw. Roman knew Adrian would leave as soon as he possibly could without upsetting anyone, if not sooner. He had the body language of a man holding himself in check, but desperately wanting to move, like a runner in the starting blocks.

Sarah gripped Roman's hand. She looked at her broken nephew, then said in a low voice that Adrian could not hear, "He has to go, Roman. His life ended in that grave and he'll not stay a minute longer than he has to. Only respect for you is keeping him here this long."

"I know," Roman responded, in an equally low and husky voice. "You're right. I should make it easier on him, not harder. Let's pack him some food, maybe a few things he wouldn't think to take along." Still holding Sarah's hand, Roman raised his voice a little and said to Adrian. "Come by the house before you go. We'll be wanting to say goodbye." They turned and walked away.

Adrian heard Roman's parting words with relief. He thought, "They aren't going to argue with me anymore. Good. I can be miles from here by dark." He looked around him slowly, his ability to see the world around him partially coming back to him. Everyone had left him to be alone at the grave. It was the first time in days that no one was hovering over him, smothering him with well-intentioned concern. He knelt on one knee beside the grave. He remained there, silent, head bowed. He did not hear the mockingbirds. After a long while, he went home.

In his and Alice's house he impatiently packed a few things, barely aware of what he was choosing to take. Shouldering his pack, he picked up his shotgun and walked out for the last time, leaving the door open behind him. He had been in the house less than five minutes. Leaving the door open was a statement to his community: they were welcome to what they could use, including the house itself. He would not be back soon. If he ever returned, he would not enter it again. He didn't look back.

As promised, he strode swiftly to Roman and Sarah's home and walked in. In his entire life he had not once knocked on their door, they would have been insulted if he had. They had packed him a supply of pemmican, coffee, salt, and a few other odds and ends. Sarah had stopped by Adrian's house and picked out a locket that Alice had frequently worn. Alice's favorite. She placed it in his hand and closed his fingers around it. Sarah sobbed, turned, and fled to the bedroom, broken hearted at Adrian's pain and departure.

Roman gave Adrian a firm hug and then stood in the doorway, watching his nephew through blurry eyes as he disappeared into the woods. Adrian would be a deeply changed man when they next met.

CHAPTER 2

HE LOOKED DOWN AT HIS compass, turning it slightly to ease the glare. The needle pointed northwest, right on track. Adrian noted a microwave tower two points off his bearing. Microwave towers were good navigation points. They were generally on the highest ground in the area, and aligned with one another. As long as he walked two points to the right of the tower he would be on course. He put the compass back in his pocket, eased the pack slightly on his shoulders, and walked on.

It had been three weeks since he had left Fort Brazos. He was intent on getting to the Rocky Mountains before winter, but he had plenty of time. Adrian was drifting, physically and mentally, while grieving. He had found that Roman's warning was right; the grief was deepening daily with no bottom in sight. At first he had been moving rapidly, intent on increasing the distance between him and Alice's grave, literally trying to out-run the pain. After several days he slowed, realizing it didn't matter where he was; the grief was inside him, not back there in the dirt.

He found the only thing that could stop his mind from

continually revolving around the pain was to pay close attention to everything outside him. If he looked closely at the ground in front of him, the vegetation and animals, details in the distance, he could distract himself. He had thus become an almost insanely keen observer. But observation alone was not enough. He also discovered that if he became involved in the world around him, it helped even more. Adrian decided to live as much like a Paleolithic traveler as possible. That would require his full attention. He began by looking for flint.

While at Fort Brazos, Adrian had spent many afternoons studying Roman's survivalist library. There he had found a small paperback book on flint knapping. Reading the book, he discovered that glass could be worked the same way and with the same tools as flint. He had practiced on broken glass and then found some flint in the river bed and worked it. He wasn't very good at it, but he could rough out the tools he needed. They weren't attractive like the prehistoric flint tips he had seen, but they were functional. Central Texas was rich with artifacts. Roman had taught him what worked flint looked like, and that where he found one worked piece he was likely to find many others. He learned that usually, flint was briefly worked at the source where it was found, then thoroughly worked at a campsite.

He observed the landscape closely as he walked. Thinking "Where to camp tonight? Near water, above the flash flood line. Somewhere with firewood, and a view of the surrounding area. Rain's likely from the look of those clouds, I'll need something sheltered from weather." Adrian drew in a deep breath, tasting the scent of distant rain. His eyes scanned back and forth across the landscape as he walked. The softening light was another rain signal. One spot nearby looked to have the best possibilities.

It was uphill from a grove of cottonwood trees. "Cottonwood trees often mean water," he thought. To his west there was a steep cliff face of limestone, breaking the prevailing wind that blew from the North West. Perhaps there would be a cave or overhang. Satisfied that it would be as good a place as he was likely to find, he veered toward it.

Adrian knew that any good camping spots he came across today had probably already been used as such for thousands of years by primitive man. He had discovered some that showed signs of having been used by primitive man for tens of thousands of years. The amount of time they had been out of use until the grid had dropped was only a brief pause on the larger scale. The most enduring signs were flakes from flint working. When he found a good source of flint, primitive man would stop and briefly work the flint at the source. These quarries were not generally great camping places, so the stone worker would chip off large blanks of flint. These were easy to carry and work on later, in a better place.

Adrian avoided roads and towns and houses. The further northwest he travelled the fewer of them there were. He realized he was seeing the same contours and streams that ancient travelers had seen while on foot. He had found a rhythm to the travelling. A day's journey from one good, previously used campsite fairly often led to another good campsite. It was as though he was travelling an ancient trail, with regular stopping places along the way. It made sense to him; his travelling pace would be about the same as the ancients'. It seemed that at the end of each day he would find where they, too, had stopped and camped.

The campsites were usually the place where those flint blanks were worked. The hunters or travelers would work blanks into spearheads and other tools while sitting around the fire. The pieces that were worked off of the blanks, and the broken pieces that didn't work out, were left on the ground. They never deteriorated, although they would be slowly scattered and covered up by time and erosion. Adrian often found useful tools, sometimes excellent points, at these camp sites. He was never sure if the whole pieces were accidentally left behind, or if the stone workers had a higher standard of quality than Adrian was able to discern from the leavings. Regardless, these places had become treasure troves of once-again useful implements.

He reached the cliff face an hour before sunset. He wiped sweat from his forehead with his sleeve while he looked around. Walking about slowly and stirring rocks with a long stick, he spotted several flint flakes and a complete flint knife blade. "Bingo! I'll stay here a couple of days and see what I can work up in the way of tools." The thought was punctuated by the sound of thunder rumbling overhead.

He looked over the spot and, as he suspected from the flint workings, discovered the reason this was an old, longtime camp; there was an overhang of rock ledge jutting out from the cliff face. He could see the blackened stone where eons of fires had been built. He could almost smell the smoke of past fires; closing his eyes he imagined the voices of men telling stories around the fire at night. Dropping his pack, he gathered enough dry wood to last the night, stacking it neatly under the ledge. Then he walked down to the cottonwoods.

There he found a spring-fed creek. Cottonwood trees are water loving, and usually grow near a source, although sometimes it is buried down deep. He watched the water for a few minutes. He caught and threw a grasshopper into the water and it was immediately taken by a fish. Adrian guessed he had enough time to build a trap and set it before the storm came in. He cut eight small saplings the size of his little finger and about five feet long. He cut them with the flint blade he had just found—it was naturally serrated, amazingly sharp, and worked well.

Stripping the green bark from the saplings in thin strips, he made crude cordage. He was pressed for time by the encroaching storm, so he simply rolled the bark strips rapidly between his palms to break the fibers loose, then twisted the bark. He cut four smaller saplings, about a quarter of the size of his little finger. He tied them into hoops with the cordage, then using the other saplings he made a basket-style fish trap with inverted ends that had smaller openings. He made it swiftly; it wasn't his first fish trap.

Adrian set the trap in a narrow spot in the creek, a place where any fish moving up or down stream would almost have to pass through. Rocks were used to weigh it down in place, including a large rock inside of it. He gathered more rocks and made funnels into each end of the trap, forcing more fish to come through. He would check it in a little while. Adrian returned to the cliff face and saw where hip and shoulder holes had already been dug out of the caliche earth. He collected cedar boughs and laid them over the area. It made a comfortable enough bed.

While collecting firewood he had also collected fire-starting materials. Fine, dry grass, an old bird's nest blown out of a tree, some dry milkweed stems that he crushed. Using his magnesium fire starter, he had a fire going in no time. "I'm cheating," he thought to himself. "I should be using a fire bow. I'll work on that soon."

He went back to the fish trap while there was still enough light to see and found two small fish in it. It would barely do, but...he walked up the stream a hundred yards and then began walking back down towards the trap, hitting the water with a tree limb. He was scaring the fish toward and hopefully into the trap. When he checked again he had two more fish. Lightning flashed. A few drops started to fall. Adrian emptied and reset the trap, and double timed back to the cliff.

He made two small columns of rocks on either side of the fire, then set a large, flat rock atop them so it was straddling the coals. From the looks of it this stone had been used this way before; more of the ancients' craft left behind. He poured some water on it to clean it. When the coals had heated the flat rock enough, he split the fish open and laid them on it to cook. He ate the fish with hopes of catching more during the night for the next day's breakfast. Then he settled in for the night as the storm hit with full force. Wind whipped and rain swirled over the cliff. Hail scattered the ground for a few minutes. It grew cold. He had kept his mind busy, up to that moment, but the grief came crashing back in. It rolled like thunder through his chest. He played her harmonica, its sound drifting out and melting into the storm.

CHAPTER 3

T HE STORM CONTINUED, RAINING HARD, then softly, then hard again, through the night. Lightning flashed rapidly as thunder rumbled across the valley below. Adrian was exhausted from grief and his attempts to avoid it. The storm lost intensity toward morning as the ground cooled. By dawn, the storm had been over for an hour.

Adrian hadn't slept well, but on awakening was free of the grief for two or three seconds. Then the painful memory flooded back into him. It was the worst time of the day, that moment when he remembered. The moment after that brief awakening moment when his mind had forgotten. A fresh breeze blew up the hill side; it was clean and carried the odors of the wet grass and dirt it had brushed across to reach him. He knew the fish trap would have been washed away by the downpour in the night. Adrian stood and stretched long and hard. He stirred the coals and placed fresh wood on the fire to get it started.

The sun rose as Adrian made the last of the coffee that Sarah had packed for him. He would leave the small coffee pot here; he would not have a use for it now, not if he was going to live primitively. He would need to learn how to make a cooking pot. He had read of the techniques but had never practiced. This camping spot would eventually draw someone to it. They might find the coffee pot invaluable. If not, they could leave it for the next travelers to come along. The aroma of fresh coffee aroused a final regret about leaving Fort Brazos behind. Adrian drank the coffee, savoring it as long as he could.

He concentrated his focus on each sip, rolling it on his tongue before finally swallowing it. He finished the pot, rinsed it and set it upside down with a heavy rock on top of it and a small rock underneath one edge, ready for the next wanderer. In the meantime it might as well supply a few field mice with shelter; propped up slightly as it was they could shelter inside. He would, however, take his shotgun with him. It would rust and become useless if left without maintenance. Maybe someday he would find someone to give it to. Until then it would be carried as baggage.

He was sure the trap was gone, but a man didn't rely on simply his thoughts where traps were concerned. It would be the worst kind of mistake to leave a trap untended. Traps that were no longer being used had to be dismantled. No need to be cruel to animals out of laziness. They were just trying to survive another day, the same as he was. The rain had swollen the creek into a muddy torrent. The trap would have come apart in that current, broken down into simple sticks again, releasing any fish it might have held. Adrian could find no sign of it.

His stomach growled ferociously as he walked back to camp. He had two choices: go hungry or eat pemmican. He chose hunger. He was a long way from being in trouble as far as food was concerned; better to save the pemmican for emergency use. The hunger pangs helped keep his mind focused. "Makes me a better hunter" he thought to himself. As he took the fire apart and let the coals die he contemplated on his internal words "Makes me a better hunter". "True words," he thought "A hungry hunter is a better hunter." But what interested him the most was that he used words less often when thinking these days.

When he was with other people, he thought in words all the time. When Adrian left Fort Brazos he was thinking in words. The longer he had been away from other people, the less often he used words to think with." Adrian considered this for a while. The camp was clean, the fire out, the coffee pot propped up. He left the pine boughs where they were. The map unfolded easily and Adrian re-checked his position. He had intended to stay for a couple of days, but he was restless and wanted to keep moving, to stay distracted. He took out his compass and walked around the cliff face. He spotted a large tree on a ridge in the distance that was in the right direction and began walking towards it.

He was out of food except for the pemmican so walking now meant hunting. He moved more slowly and quietly. He watched the ground ahead of him for signs of small game, and the further distance for glimpses of larger kills. Occasionally on this trip he had come across feral cows. They would have been easy to kill, but Adrian had passed on them. They were too large for one man to make efficient use of without freezers to hold the meat. He could have killed them, taken the best parts for immediate use and made jerky of more of it, but he would still have had to leave over half the animal behind, and he wouldn't do that. Someday those feral cows were going to be important.

Deer were altogether different. Deer were considerably smaller; he could utilize an entire deer, although he would have to stop and camp to prepare it. Since he was in no hurry that was fine with him. Just as long as he could stay busy. He had been shooting game up to this point, and still had plenty of ammunition left, but now he was going to hunt like a primitive man. He would have to learn new techniques. Or rather he thought, relearn old techniques.

Adrian found a stick the right size and shape to make a throwing stick and carried it with him as he walked. Throwing sticks were among the first hunting tools. They were short, heavy sticks that could be thrown at small game, stunning the animal long enough for the hunter to pounce on it. Boomerangs were crafted throwing sticks designed to be thrown at small game. That design had the aerodynamic quirk of curved flight. North American throwing sticks were usually about two feet long and straight with a knob on one end. The end-over-end flight path of a throwing stick widened its hitting radius to the full length of the stick, making it more effective than throwing a rock. A rock would work, but required a great deal more accuracy because its striking radius was only the size of the rock itself. A throwing stick worked better.

As a child Adrian had made several slings for rock throwing. They were deadly when the rock hit the target, but that was a low percentage proposition. In his experience the sling's accuracy was a myth; they required months of practice and one had to find a supply of rocks the same size and density in order to have a chance. Even then, he missed his target far more often than he hit it.

They also required time to load, swing, and throw, giving the game animal time to alert and run. But with the stick he carried, all he had to do was pull his arm back and throw. It was more efficient, even though limited in range.

Atlatls were much better, but required long reeds for their darts. He was travelling through country that didn't offer reeds, but when he did find some he would make one.

Adrian threw the stick at a bush that was on the edge of his throwing range, but missed it by inches. He retrieved the stick, walked back to where he had thrown it, and tried again, and again, and again until he was hitting the bush every time. He continued walking.

Adrian flushed a bird at his feet and threw the stick at it, missing. An hour later he startled a jack rabbit, but it was beyond his range. An hour before dusk he jumped another jack rabbit, closer this time. The stick was in the air before he realized he had thrown it, and it smacked the rabbit in the back. Adrian was running as soon as he threw, sensing that it would hit. The rabbit lost its footing for a second when the stick made contact with it, but that was all Adrian needed. He grabbed the rabbit and broke its neck instantly, as humane a kill as he could. Adrian had dinner.

It was time to choose a campsite. The weather looked good, so he chose a spot above a nearby creek. He took the rabbit to the creek and removed its skin, then opened the stomach with his flint blade and removed the entrails and organs. He rinsed the rabbit's stomach cavity out, then opened the entrails and squeezed out the contents carefully. He split the entrails lengthwise and rinsed them out, then put them back into the stomach cavity and rolled the dressed rabbit back up inside the skin. Adrian gathered wood for a fire, and because he had not built a fire bow, started it with his magnesium fire-starting tool.

Cultural blindness had caused many people to starve; history books were replete with stories of the kind. People would refuse to eat certain items that were necessary, and die as a result. Blind stupidity. Adrian had been trained in survival by the smartest and most experienced tutors in the world. They had taught about rabbit starvation. During the opening of the west, settlers had died of starvation with their bellies full of rabbit. The problem was they ate only the lean meat of the rabbit. Their upbringing, their culture, had not prepared them for the need to eat the rest of the animal. What they had not known was that man needed not just protein, they needed fat as well. Without fat in his diet, he eventually died. He had been taught that each animal carried the correct ratio of fat to protein that a man needed. It was simple really: each animal had to have fat in it to survive just as a man did, and if it was healthy, the ratio of fat to protein was there. The problem for the settlers had been where the fat was located. What they failed to comprehend was that the whole animal had to be eaten. Brains, entrails, organs, and bone marrow. All of it was necessary to survival.

Adrian knew that Stone Age man had learned to make cooking pots out of tree bark and animal skins. Adrian would eventually do that as well, but he didn't have time for that right now, or the materials at hand. He roasted the rabbit on one spit over the fire, head still on. He speared the organs on other small sharpened sticks and placed them over the fire, and wrapped the entrails around another stick and placed it over the fire. He carefully tended each stick, turning it as necessary until every piece had been cooked enough to kill any bacteria or parasites. That would happen when the meat had reached 180 degrees at the bone. Adrian gauged this by how the meat began to pull away from the ends of the bones.

He ate all the meat, entrails, and organs, then cracked open the head and ate the cooked brain. He put the bones back into the fire for a few more minutes. Rabbit bones didn't take long. Once he had cooked the marrow inside the bones he removed them from the fire and split them open, scraping out and eating the marrow. There wasn't much of it, but every bit helped. Adrian would have preferred to stew the rabbit parts all together in a pot, and would soon be making a pot to do that with. It would be simpler, tastier, and less wasteful of the nutrients.

As he cooked the meat on the spits he noted the fluids dripping off the meat. Those fluids contained nutrients. In a stew those nutrients stayed in the broth. The boiling water also removed nutrients from the bone cells that were otherwise impossible to remove. When stewing, the bones were removed from the meat, split to expose the marrow, and placed back in the pot. Altogether a better way to utilize everything the animal had to offer.

Again, the work of survival had helped a little. He lay looking up at the stars for a long time, trying and failing to not feel the pain, before exhausted sleep overtook him. He slept the sleep of the mentally exhausted, not the physically exhausted. As he lay there, he had no idea that the next day would bring people into his life again, if only briefly.

CHAPTER 4

ADRIAN ATE SOME OF THE rabbit that he had reserved for breakfast. He had learned morning hunger could be intense, but easily resolved with a few bites of protein. He knew that it was better to have a small dinner and a large breakfast than the reverse, but he also knew that the best plan was to eat when hungry, if possible.

Walking along looking for more game to throw his stick at, he spotted a Bois D'Arc tree, also known as Osage Orange. They were easy to recognize because of their large, green fruit the size of softballs. Later in the year they would turn yellow. He had grown up around these trees and called them horse-apple trees, as did most people in his area. The trees were once planted in close knit rows and as they grew, their entangled thorny branches made natural fences and wind breaks. The trees had been a popular item to plant as the west was occupied until the advent of barbed wire. They had grown well in the Southern and Western climates. It was the favored wood for making long bows by the original inhabitants of the continent.

Adrian chose a long, straight branch of the right diameter, about the size of a small woman's wrist. One with no side branches to create knots. He cut the limb with his flint knife; it took almost an hour to cut the tough wood. For now he would use the limb as a staff, a handy tool and weapon in itself. When the wood eventually seasoned he would make a long bow of it. He walked on with the throwing stick in his left, dominant hand and the staff in his right.

It was time to make a fire bow, so he had chosen a burled piece of the Bois D'Arc wood to make the cup that he would use to hold down the twirling stick. The burl was a tight, hard, grained wood that fit his hand. He used another longer piece for the bow. For the twirling and bottom sticks he watched for a softer wood, eventually settling on pieces of dry cottonwood for this. Adrian pulled leaves off of Sotol plants, they would provide cordage materials. He also replaced his throwing stick with a green piece of Bois D'Arc because it was heavier and would make a harder impact. With a bit of work with his flint knife he soon had it tuned up.

Adrian had been loosely following a river and had entered the Palo Duro Canyon. The beauty of the place was evident, though he didn't think about it on a conscious level. He had been lulled by weeks of walking alone. He smelled smoke, and went into stealth mode smoothly and efficiently. He stopped moving, frozen in place while assessing what he could see and smell. Motion drew the eye faster than anything else. Very slowly he lowered himself into a cross-legged sitting position. This put his eyes above the brush to where he could see around him but kept his profile low. He began to slowly rotate his head, shifting his position quietly so he could scan around him in a complete circle. He saw no one.

The smell of smoke was coming from ahead of him, its source probably from a good distance away. He was being overly cautious, but why not? Adrian stood and quickly walked over to a grove of mesquite trees, then disappeared into them. He waited and watched from inside the trees but still saw no sign of people, just the faint odor of the smoke alerted him. He stalked slowly into the wind, following the smoke scent.

It took him two hours to travel the distance he would normally have covered in half an hour, but no detail slipped past his intense scrutiny. This type of concentration was tiring. It fatigued the mind and muscles. It was difficult to remember to keep the muscles relaxed when the mind was so focused on external matters, and the muscles tended to stay tightened unnecessarily. Knowing this, he took breaks each hour. He would sit down with his back to a tree or boulder, in some hidden place, close his eyes and deliberately relax his entire body. He would perform a brief meditation, allowing his mind to go blank. It was a simple technique he had learned overseas.

Close the eyes and clear the mind of thought by paying attention to breathing. Within minutes he would be in a deeply relaxed physical state, but his mind was still keenly aware of his surroundings. He would get as much rest in fifteen minutes as he would from a long nap. While in the meditative state his senses were hyper-alert to any change. He was far from unaware of his surroundings when he rested this way.

Adrian found the source of the smoke. He lay in hiding, watching six people around the fire. There were three men and three women, a trio of couples judging by their behavior. They were in their mid to late twenties, and they had the look of people who had been on the edge of starvation for a long time. They had a .22 rifle leaning against a tree. No one paid it any attention and Adrian had a hunch they were out of ammunition. It was mid-day and they were cooking four small fish, a paltry meal for one, merely a tease for six people. No one seemed to be in charge of the group because no one seemed to receive any deference from anyone else. After half an hour's observation, Adrian knew they were no threat to him. Quite the opposite.

He stood up, stretched, and then walked toward them. He played a quick upbeat blues riff on his harmonica as he approached, hoping the music would signal his friendliness. The six people immediately panicked. The women withdrew behind the men who picked up crude spears that were essentially long, sharpened sticks. One of them picked up the rifle and pointed it at Adrian, but didn't work the bolt or the safety. They group was skittish. One of the men, the tallest one, replied, "Stay where you are. Who are you? What are you doing here? What do you want?"

"No need to be alarmed," Adrian said. "I'll not cause anyone harm. I have my own food and don't need or want yours. I am recently widowed and travelling to the mountains. That should cover all the bases. I smelled your fire and haven't talked to anyone in over a month."

Adrian smiled. He knew it would take time for them to absorb what he had said, and that he might have to repeat himself several times before they relaxed. He was used to this reaction. Just the sight of his six-foot plus height and heavily muscled body intimidated many men. There was something about him that caused men to instinctively understand that Adrian was an extremely capable fighter. He was used to the reaction. He moved with an athletic grace and an extraordinary confidence that caused subconscious respect. He was also aware that women were attracted to him wherever he went, and that their mates sensed and resented that attraction. That resentment was dangerous and something Adrian tried to allay. Hence his introduction as recently widowed.

"I smelled your smoke. I haven't seen anyone in over a month. I thought it would be a nice break to stop and visit before getting on my way again. I don't want anything, other than conversation. My name is Adrian. I am on my way to the mountains. I left our village on the Brazos six weeks ago."

"I'm Roger," one of the men said. He casually pointed the rifle at the ground between them instead of at Adrian, which was a good sign. "We're from Amarillo. We were out here camping when the grid went down. Of course we didn't know the grid went down; we just saw the northern lights. When we tried to go back we found out what happened. There were riots in the city, so we came back here. Been here ever since. You got any food you want to share? The women could use a bite or two."

Adrian was naturally averse to giving away food. The pemmican he had would barely feed these six people one meal, but for him it was a life-saving bundle. "No food that I care to share, no. However, there is food all around you. If you'd like I can show you a couple of things that would make your lives easier." With that, Adrian moved forward. It was time to take charge and stop standing around. Adrian strode forward with total confidence, his hand out in front of him to shake.

Roger reacted as Adrian hoped he would. Still carrying inside him the city dweller's instinct to avoid confrontation; Roger put his hand out and shook. The ice was broken. To further disarm the men, Adrian took a seat by the fire, placing him lower than them—a clear signal he didn't intend to make any threatening actions. Adrian laid his staff down beside him, completely flat on the ground. The symbolism of his body language was deliberate on his part. It would instinctively be understood as a non-threatening action.

Adrian had thought talking to them might be a diversion, but realized even as he sat down that he really didn't want to be there with them. He already wanted to be alone again. However, he had committed himself and would see it through. The six people gathered around, eager to talk. They hadn't seen a friendly stranger since the grid dropped. They'd had a few violent and harsh confrontations after the solar storm, but those people had died or disappeared quickly. These six were starved for more than food.

Adrian picked up a small stick and stirred the coals for a moment. "My wife died just over six weeks ago. We were married a year and a half. She was a doctor, had set up a hospital at our village, Fort Brazos. She contracted a disease from a patient. The patient died the day after he came in to the hospital. Alice died later, alone, in self-imposed quarantine. In order to keep busy I took on a trip to see the mountains. If I find good people I aim to tell them about Fort Brazos, how to get there. It's a good place to live, with good people living there. They need more good people." Adrian could feel sympathy coming off the women like heat waves as they heard in his tone how much he had loved Alice, and how heartbroken he was. The men barely paid attention to that part of his story, focused instead on the fact that Fort Brazos sounded like a good place to live.

Roger looked at the other five in his group. They all seemed to expect him to do the talking. Adrian noticed this and realized that Roger was their leader; it was just that none of them, including Roger, had figured it out. "You said there was food around us we aren't seeing. I would be interested in you showing that to us, if you would. It has been a long time since we had a decent meal."

Adrian stood up and said, "Roger, you come with me. The rest of you stay here. Build an underground oven while we're gone. Dig a pit about the size of a large washtub. Line it with rocks on the bottom and sides. Pile up a large pile of flat rocks nearby. Build a hot fire in the rock-lined pit. We want to see a good bed of hot coals in it when we get back." Adrian issued these commands in a normal tone of voice, implying that Roger was involved in the command; it was a tone that expected nothing short of complete obedience. Without checking for compliance, he walked off, Roger following.

When they were out of sight and hearing, Adrian stopped, slightly startling Roger. Adrian looked Roger square in the eyes and said, "You have to lead these people. They want you to, but they don't know how to say it. They need leadership. I expect you to take them to Fort Brazos, where you'll all be better off. It'll be a tough trip, but you can do it. I'm going to show you a few things that will make it easier. I'm going to show you, then you show them. It'll be simpler for me to teach one person than six, and it will put you naturally into the leadership role with them. First lesson in survival is the one I just gave you. Every tribe needs a leader. You have to step up to it now." Adrian started walking again without waiting for a reply.

Roger was again startled when Adrian stopped for seemingly no reason. Adrian pointed to a Sotol plant and said, "See this plant? It has three immediately valuable uses. You can make strong cordage and baskets from it, and you can eat it." Taking out his flint knife Adrian trimmed the leaves and collected the heart. "This is edible after it has been cooked for 36 to 48 hours at high temperatures. If you try to eat it before that it will make you sick. When cooked it tastes like nutty molasses syrup. It has a lot of nutrition. These plants are everywhere around here; they were a mainstay food of the native people. I'm going to wait here for you. You go back to the camp and tell two of them how to collect these and have them collect as many as they can, then trim and save the leaves and hearts. More would be better. Now go, and hurry back."

Roger left and Adrian seriously considered leaving a map drawn in the dirt and heading off on his own again. He was not enjoying this encounter. The coupled-ness of the six made his grief more unbearable than before.

CHAPTER 5

ROGER RETURNED TWENTY MINUTES LATER, having issued the instructions. He noticed that Adrian appeared to be almost indifferent to his presence. Adrian stood mute for a long moment, then said, "I'll show you how to make cordage and baskets tonight. Right now I want you to show me how you catch fish."

Roger smiled and pulled a piece of fishing line with a hook on it from his shirt pocket. "We came here to camp and brought a fishing pole with us. The pole was broken long ago, but we removed the line and made several individual fishing lines from it. We tied them to limbs hanging over the water and caught fish. We lost most of them over time and only have two left."

"I thought it would be something like that," Adrian said. "Look here, you're going to starve on fish if that's all you have to eat. But I'll show you how to trap fish. You can make the traps wherever you are and almost always catch fish." With that, Adrian walked to the river's edge. He found a willow tree and removed several branches. He quickly built a fish trap while explaining to Roger each step of the process. Then he had Roger build a trap while

Adrian explained to him how to choose the best places to put the traps, and how to improve those places.

They took the two traps and Adrian watched as Roger applied the lesson, placing the traps and building rock walls to improve their potential. Adrian searched the shallow water, found what he was looking for, and called Roger over. "See that dark line there? It looks sort of like a twig in the mud, right? That is a fresh water mussel." Adrian reached down, scooping his fingers into the mud. He swished his hand back and forth in the water to clean the mud off the mussel, then straightened and handed it to Roger.

"Look how he closed his shell. They sit buried in the mud with only a small portion of their edge showing with their shell slightly open, filtering the water for food. That's the best way to see them. Where you find one you usually find many. Raccoons love to eat these and you'll notice the empty shells around here, and the raccoon tracks. Those are good indications of where to start looking. Let's dig up a bunch to take back with us for dinner tonight. First, though, we will break a few open and put them in the fish traps. They make good bait."

Roger and Adrian dug up over a hundred mussels and put them in Roger's pack. They returned to the camp to find the pit had been built and a fire going well inside of it. The others had gathered twenty of the Sotol plants. Adrian inspected one and showed them how to trim the leaves off; leaving what looked something like a misshaped pineapple. When the fire burned down Adrian began laying the flat stones from the pile on top of the still burning coals. The layer of rock was placed over the coals, then the Sotol was placed on the rocks. More rocks were placed over the Sotol until they were well covered.

Another fire was built on top of these stones until they were well heated. This created an underground hot stone oven. Adrian had the women make mud and plaster the top rocks an inch thick after raking off the coals, Then he had them cover the whole thing with a mound of loose soil to hold in the heat.

"I'll be gone when these are cooked, so listen up," Adrian said. "Wait at least thirty six hours, but forty eight is better. Remove the cooked plants and allow them to cool off enough so you can handle them. They will be sticky and pulpy. You can eat some right then. Not too much until your stomachs have adjusted to their richness; they contain a lot of sugar and other carbohydrates. The rest of them you pound into cakes or patties and dry in the sun. As long as you keep them dry they'll last for months and can be eaten cold. They make great trail food. I recommend you continue to collect, cook, and prepare as much of them as you can carry before you head for Fort Brazos. You should be able to carry enough to get there and not have to depend on hunting on the way. I'll show you how to carry them."

Taking a handful of the Sotol leaves, Adrian wove a mat quickly, splicing in more leaves as he expanded it. He set that aside, took more leaves, and pounded the fibers loose with his throwing stick and a large rock. He rolled the fibers between his palms to break them loose from each other, then demonstrated how to make cordage. When he had a length of the cordage ready he tied the woven matt into a crude but functional basket. "You can make pack baskets with a bit of trial and error. You can make all kinds of useful things from these plants, and they grow all over the place. You can survive on these plants fairly well, although you really want to have protein and fat in your diet too."

Adrian took some more leaves and cordage and quickly made a sandal. "You can make these easily and quickly. They don't stand up long, but carry extras with you and you can travel many miles without hurting your feet."

Adrian stood and removed the mussels from Roger's pack. Adrian put some of the mussels on the campfire. "These are going to cook quickly. They'll steam inside the shell, and the shell will open up as a result. When they are cooked, scoop them out of the shells and eat them. Always cook them thoroughly or you may get parasites." After a few minutes, Adrian removed a half dozen, then sat down and began eating them to show them how it was done. The six were apt students and soon cooking and gorging themselves on mussels.

"Okay, everybody, to the river to collect more for tonight. Hurry now before it gets dark." They feasted on mussels and fish that night; the traps had already caught several.

The next morning the traps yielded more fish, and they all spent time collecting, then eating, more mussels. The men and women looked less stressed than when Adrian had arrived. The realization of how much food was in the river, and how easily it could be harvested, did a tremendous job of improving their outlook. Adrian was happy about that, but itching to get moving. However, he still had a full day of teaching.

Adrian felt like one of his survival instructors must have felt. He explained, "There are two reasons you were starving. One is ignorance and the other is blindness. An example of ignorance is you didn't know that you can eat Sotol plants, or about the other benefits it has. Now that you know you realize you have a source of food. Blindness is not lack of sight in this case, but culturally induced blindness. You've noticed how many grasshoppers are around here. You've used them for fish bait. Yet you never made the connection with eating them yourselves. In much of the world, people eat insects on a routine basis, even when they aren't starving. They like them. You find the idea repugnant, even now when you have been so close to dying for lack of food.

"So who is right? The people who eat grasshoppers and live or the people that don't eat grasshoppers and die? They're easy to catch and nutritious. Catch them and pull off the wings and legs; you won't digest those and they are difficult to swallow. Roast the grasshoppers on a hot, flat stone. Never eat them raw or you'll get parasites. Never eat any animal or insect raw. You don't need parasites on top of everything else you have to deal with. Crickets, waterbugs, tarantulas, ants, termites, scorpions, snakes, lizards, snails, earthworms, termite larvae, and grub worms are all excellent sources of fuel for your body. These are all around you nearly all the time. They are proven survival foods and considered delicacies in many cultures.

"Roger, come with me. The rest of you gather more Sotol and prepare another oven. You're going to want to have a lot of it on hand when you leave. Catch grasshoppers and crickets, too." Roger jumped up and eagerly followed Adrian out of the camp. They walked along quietly, Adrian watching the ground, looking for what he was sure he would find. In an hour he had discovered a flint outcrop.

He showed it to Roger. "I'm not very good at knapping yet, but I can make useful tools, although crude by our ancestor's standards." It only took a few minutes for Adrian to demonstrate and explain to Roger what he knew of knapping.

"Okay, you know as much about that as I do now. You'll have to learn by doing. Someone in your group will be better than the rest of you, I suggest when you find out who that is and put him or her to work at it, making tools for everyone. You can work glass the same way; it pressure flakes off exactly like flint, and is easier to work with—it has no fault lines in it. The bottom part of a glass jar or bottle is a good thickness to work with.

"Now we need to make atlatls. See those reeds over there? That's a good place to start." Adrian walked over to the reeds and cut a dozen of them down. Then he walked back to the river and placed them under water with rocks on them to hold them down.

"We need these to soften up a little, makes straightening them easier. An atlatl is a lever that makes it possible to throw a mini-spear with enough force to kill a deer." Looking around at the pieces of driftwood available he selected two that would make decent atlatl sticks. He carved them into shape with his flint knife blade. When they were in the shape he wanted them, he used cordage to make the thumb loops. He then removed the reeds from the water and shaped and scraped them into arrows, which were actually called darts.

"You can put flint tips on these when you have made some that will work," he explained to Roger. "The tips don't have to be perfect arrowheads, but they do need to be pointed and sharp. In the meantime we can use sharpened pieces of hardwood and bind them to the ends." Adrian used green willow to make twelve sharpened, short points and bound them to the reeds. Look here, this is how these work." Adrian then demonstrated. Roger and Adrian practiced on a target until they had found their range and accuracy potential.

"Let's go hunting."

Roger was a natural hunter. He proved adept at killing small game with the atlatl Adrian had made. While they were hunting, Adrian explained to him how to hunt deer and wild boar. He explained what their habits were, how to pattern their trails, when and where to look for them.

"The darts don't kill them on the spot. It causes them to bleed to death which takes time. The worst thing you can do is start trailing them right away. That causes them to keep running and makes them harder to find. Instead wait half an hour. During that time, if not chased, they will usually hole up in the thickest brush they can find and lay down. Laying down, their muscles will stiffen up as they bleed out. You won't have to trail them as far and the blood trail will be easier to follow."

He described where Fort Brazos was and the best way to get there. He taught Roger about traveling carefully and avoiding strangers and a dozen other useful pieces of information. Adrian had begun to think that Roger was a useful person, as high a compliment as a man could ask for in the post-grid days. He was intelligent and a quick study, only needing basic instruction before he was ready to tackle a task. Adrian gave him a crash course in survival skills during that one hunting trip. There wasn't time to spread it out.

He demonstrated how to set a variety of snares, and the best kind of places to set them. "Set snares every evening near your camp. Check them as soon as you can see the next morning. Remove all the snares and take them with you; never leave a snare behind to kill and waste food. It's wrong, don't do it."

They returned to the camp with three jack rabbits, a

possum, and four rattlesnakes. Eyes lit up at the sight of meat. They had been busy as well, collecting and preparing more Sotol, mussels, and fish, and creating another underground oven. They had been roasting and snacking on grasshoppers. Everyone was busy and productive. Their morale was excellent. The change in this group in two days was gratifying. Adrian believed that they had enough skills and now enough knowledge among them to survive. They had good attitudes and definite leadership. Better yet, they had a goal, a place to get to: Fort Brazos.

Adrian called over Roger and handed him his shotgun and all of the ammunition for it. Roger looked at Adrian curiously.

"Where I'm going, the way I'm going, I don't need this," Adrian said. "Take if for defense, not hunting. Fire it only if you have to—in defense of you and your people. Then as soon as you can, get away from that area. Do not use it for hunting; you have silent means for that. Shooting a gun is an announcement of where you are to anyone within earshot. The good guys aren't going to come running to see what's up, but the bad guys will. They'll hear the shot and think of it as an opportunity to steal food, or to kill.

"They'll also automatically know that you're armed, so they won't come at you in the open. They'll be sneaky about it. Shooting this is an invitation to disaster, so only shoot it to avoid a disaster. Then get away from that area as fast and stealthily as you can. You might run right into the bad guys if you're not careful. Keep in mind they may be coming from the direction you are heading. Promise me that if you take this, you'll do as I say."

"Sure, absolutely. But are you sure you want to give it

away, that you don't need it?"

"I'm positive."

Adrian looked at this group with a stirring of pride in what they had accomplished in so short a time. "Listen up! Ladies, there is one more thing I want to show you. If your men will allow, I want you to follow me."

The men looked startled, but having given their trust to Adrian they allowed it with silent nods.

"We'll be back in an hour or so. Come along ladies." The women, suddenly looking shy, followed him away from the camp. They did not have far to go. Adrian showed them a yucca plant.

"These can be prepared and eaten the same way as the Sotol although they need to bake even longer. They have fibers for cordage and leaves for weaving. They have something else though—shampoo. Perhaps the world's finest shampoo is right here in front of you." Adrian dug up some of the roots and carried them to the river. He pounded the roots into a pulp between rocks and showed the women how to use the juicy pulp to wash their hair. He showed them by doing it to himself.

Adrian's hair bothered him. He had been in the Army so long that short hair was his preference. Alice, however, had liked his hair long and he had let it grow to please her. It had now been close to two years since it had been cut. It was past his shoulders, and cleaning it was a pleasurable experience.

The woman laughed and hooted as they washed their hair. Adrian moved a distance back from them, standing behind some nearby bushes so they could have privacy, yet close enough to assure their safety. The women gratefully bathed themselves with frothy soap for the first time in two years. They were extremely happy. The women came out of the river with freshly washed clothes, hair and bodies. He could see the by the lightness in their steps that they were happier than they had been in a long time.

Adrian said, "Okay, Ladies, back to camp. I suspect the men will be happy to see you in such fine fettle, but you're going to suddenly start smelling them." Adrian grinned. "I suggest you tell them how to get the yucca shampoo and to go clean themselves."

When the women returned to camp the men were shocked and delighted to see the women clean and comely, and most of all, happy. While the men were off bathing Adrian drew a map by scratching it out onto a flat rock. He showed it to Roger's wife and told her to give it to Roger. Adrian also showed her Alice's locket and told her to describe it to Sarah as proof that Adrian was okay. Then, without another word, he picked up his kit and walked off, just as the men were returning. Roger followed him.

"Do you have to leave already? Don't you want to stay until morning? The Sotol will be ready then, and you can take some with you."

Adrian stopped walking and turned around. He looked Roger up and down then said, "You're a fine man, Roger, a good husband, a good provider, a natural leader, a useful man. You need me around now like you need a hole in the head. I've shown you as much as I can without moving in full time. You know enough to make it. Take care of your tribe. Tell Uncle Roman and Aunt Sarah hello for me. Tell them I'm doing fine."

Adrian abruptly turned and walked off. Roger watched him go with a feeling of foreboding, knowing that Adrian was a sad and lonely man, bent on a path of solitude, and sensing that he had a death wish.

CHAPTER 6

SOON AFTER LEAVING THE PALO Duro he entered a more desert-like landscape. This was harsh country and it was into the hot time of the year. Temperatures over one hundred degrees were now the norm. Adrian knew how to travel in the desert. He knew to carry plenty of water, to look for more as he went, and how to conserve what water he had. He made a wide-brimmed hat of Yucca leaves to shade his head and shoulders. It looked like a small sombrero or a cowboy hat with a few extra inches of brim. He covered all parts of his skin during daylight hours. Sunburn would be a disaster. Covering the skin looked hotter than exposing the skin, but it conserved body water by blocking wind and sun. Adrian had seen photographs of the Apache Indians of the late 1800's and noted that they were often fully clothed with long sleeves and pants. In fact, many of them wrapped up in blankets when out in the sun for long periods. The clothing absorbed sweat from the body, holding it close against the skin while it dried keeping the skin moister and providing a slight cooling effect as it evaporated.

Traveling at night was in some ways better than during

the day. It was cooler and used less body water. But it had its dangers; low visibility could lead to a twisted ankle or worse. A broken leg out here was a death sentence. A sprain might be survived, and it might not. This was a harsh and bitter land for the wounded. Snakes also were more prone to be out and traveling after dark, raising the risk of an encounter. Adrian did his best to find a happy medium, traveling from first light until around ten, then settling into a shady spot and sleeping until the sun had lost most of its bite, around six or so. Then he traveled again until dark.

During the night he sat by the fire occasionally playing the harmonica, and waiting. He would lay looking up at the clear night sky, the stars by the billions, clear as they could be. Eventually he would sleep until morning and start moving again.

Adrian cut down on eating, taking only one small meal per day. Water was more important than food as he crossed this environment. Digestion uses a lot of water; better to eat as little as possible, since he wasn't eating as much he didn't need to hunt as he walked. He carefully gathered prickly pears and ate them at night, burning the little needles off in his fire and lightly roasting them first. The little needles had his respect. He had encountered them as a child and could still clearly recall the pain. Prickly pears held a lot of moisture, so they were okay to eat.

He had learned in survival school that contrary to popular belief, barrel cacti were not a safe source of moisture. They were high in oxalic acid and would make the partaker extremely ill. The small fruits on top of the cactus were all right to eat in small quantities.

He also kept an eye out for signs of water. Certain types

of trees or shrubs often signaled underground water that sometimes could be reached by digging. Cottonwoods, sycamores, willows, salt cedar, and hackberry were all worth investigating. Generally they are high water consuming plants, and they root into water bearing strata. Adrian watched for these in low areas, then dug down in the lowest spot among them. When he found this water he usually let the sediment settle out and drank it without boiling it first. This water was remote from habitations and had a better than even chance of not being polluted.

Carrying water was an issue. It was difficult to construct watertight containers from what was at hand. It was also difficult to carry large quantities of it; water was heavy and awkward to travel with. Adrian had made a water storage device from the stomach of the last deer he had killed. It was a simple procedure: remove and clean the stomach, leaving a foot of entrails on top and bottom. After washing out the stomach thoroughly by submerging it in moving water he carefully turned it inside out and used his hands to separate the stomach lining from the outside membrane. The stomach lining he cooked and ate. He soaked the membrane sack in a solution made from oak bark that had been boiled to create a tannin solution.

He made sure the tannin water was inside the stomach as well as outside. After two days of soaking he stuffed it with dry grasses and leaves to hold its shape, then smoked it lightly over the fire. It was stiff, but softened with time and water inside. He did this while making jerky of the deer meat. The gut canteen would carry a two-day supply of water for him, three if he rationed it. The cordage he used to tie off the two tubes to keep the water in also served as a shoulder loop to carry it. He found that setting it against the small of his back was the best method; that way, it didn't catch on brush as much.

The water picked up some of the tannins and was a bit bitter. He knew in time the water would leach out the tannins and the bag would probably begin to deteriorate. But he also knew he would be across the desert area in a few weeks and it would last long enough. If not, he would kill another deer or an antelope and make a new one. He had read of the Apaches making tightly woven baskets and then sealing them inside with pine pitch, making them waterproof and excellent for carrying water. He was good at making baskets, and knew how to make pine pitch, but he didn't want to carry something that large and rigid along with everything else he was carrying.

With good water conservation techniques, some as simple as keeping his mouth closed and breathing through the nose, he could travel many miles without needing to replenish his water supply. Sucking prickly pear cactus pulp taken from the young leaves as he walked was a help in that regard. He chewed it lightly to obtain the mucilaginous moisture and then spit out the pulp. He could possibly travel completely across the desert doing that and not have to stop to find and drink water, but the prickly pear had a small amount of oxalic acid in it that could make him sick if he solely relied on it.

The most prevalent danger in this area was snake bite. He was cautious when he walked, using his staff to stir thick brush in front of him if he had to walk through it. Mostly people didn't die from snakebites, but it would still make him awful sick, and being sick out here was not a good idea. The bite could also become infected and gangrene could set in. Gangrene would definitely kill.

Scorpions were another worry. The small, almond-shaped ones could make a man as sick as a snake bite. Scorpions were most likely to bite in the night, when Adrian was sleeping. Each night he made a ring of rocks around his bedding. He piled the rocks two high and filled any gaps with dirt and sand. It wouldn't necessarily stop a scorpion from climbing over, but it would divert most of them around him. Before lying down to sleep he took the coals and ashes from his fire and carefully spread them on top of the rocks. He thought it might help some too.

He used willow tree bark and made a mask, using cordage to tie it behind his head, which kept him from having eyestrain and protected his face. With slits cut where his eyes were he could see just fine, but the amount of light was cut down considerably. The mask also protected his facial skin from drying out rapidly and getting sunburned. Sunburn in the desert could ultimately kill a man. He had read about Eskimos making similar eye covering devices to avoid snow blindness. It helped. He had tried leather but found it too hot.

He had also laced yucca leaves into the brim. They drooped down from the brim all around like a fringe, except in front. These further shaded his head, especially his neck, and blocked the sun. He knew he looked strange with the big hat with leaves dangling down and the bark across his face. He was aware that if he came across anyone they would be startled at his appearance. He didn't care. He didn't expect to bump into anyone and wouldn't have cared about their opinion of his clothing even if he did. He did what worked.

The moccasin boots that Alice had made would hold up for a long time, but eventually the soles would begin to wear thin. Adrian had made new soles for them from deer hide. It was a simple matter of cutting the hide to fit the bottom of his boots, then using cordage woven through holes in the edge of the deer hide, then tying them on like sandals over his boots. He made several pair and soaked them in tannin water, then dried them out over his smoke fire. Each pair lasted a long time, saving his boots from the wear. As they wore out he replaced them with another set. It was a simple fix, easy to make. He tied them on hair side out so that the hair would wear off first making them last a bit longer. They also made for silent walking.

One of the many valuable lessons Adrian had learned in the military was to take care of his feet. A man with blisters was crippled and would find himself in serious trouble. This was trouble that could be avoided with a little care. Every time Adrian stopped to rest he removed his boots and washed his feet with a bit of the water from the bag. He shook his boots out, then wiped inside them with a damp cloth to clean the inside. He let his feet air out on a regular basis and checked them thoroughly for hot spots or developing blisters. He hung the boots on brush to give them maximum exposure to whatever wind was available, airing them out. If he got a blister he would have to camp on the spot until it healed, which could take several days. It would be boring, but better than crippling his feet.

When he did stop he also worked on the flint he carried. He was steadily improving at knapping. He was making a store of different size and types of points. When he returned to hunting country he would be ahead of the curve with points. It was a good idea to have a surplus rather than run out and have to find flint in a hurry. He also kept watch for good flint while he was walking.

When he found some, he would pause to flake off blanks to carry with him to work on in camp. Learning the knapping techniques was a good distraction.

Adrian carried a backpack and several "possible" bags with him made from animal skins. Sharpening a small deer antler tine by rubbing it on a rock he used it as an awl to punch holes in the hides to sew together with strips of skin cut like shoelaces. Because he kept on the move he didn't fully tan the hides; instead he used the tannin water and smoke to semi-cure them. They were half cured and half rawhide. They dried up hard, but could be worked soft with a bit of rubbing on a blunt piece of wood or stone. They only needed to be soft enough to work with. He had these strung around on different loops of cordage and carried over his shoulder so that he could drop them instantly if he needed to move fast.

The only non-primitive equipment he still carried was his compass, bowie knife, whetstone and magnesium fire starter. He didn't use them, but he was loath to give them up. They could mean the difference between life and death at some point. Going primitive wasn't a religion, just a good distraction because it was inconvenient. If survival depended on it, he would use whatever he had, so he kept the more advanced, but highly useful equipment. He also kept Alice's locket. That he would never part with.

He traveled this way for a month, and then, slowly, the terrain and climate changed. He was still in arid country, but it was becoming mountainous. Running streams and rivers were becoming more common. The air was a little thinner, and the nights were considerably colder. The sun beat down even harder during the day through the thin air, making sunburn more of a threat. The thin air cooled rapidly as the sun went down, and it became downright frigid at night. He hadn't cured enough skins to make blankets, so he used Yucca and Sotol leaves to weave mats. He wove four mats, then sewed them together in pairs, leaving one end open on each, like large pillow cases. During the day he rolled them up and tied them to his pack. They were awkward, but light. At night he stuffed them both with dry grass and leaves, then slept on one and covered with the other. Not the best blankets he had ever slept between, but they did the job. The bottom one helped to insulate him from the ground, which in the early mornings would be cold enough to suck out his body heat.

Finally he reached the foothills of the Rockies. Here there were trees and game. He would be in elk country soon and needed to make tools sufficient to kill them. The atlatl he had carried from the Palo Duro canyon would work, but bow and arrow would work better. The staff wasn't cured enough yet to make a bow, so he looked around for something else to use. For now he would use the atlatl but with flint points instead of the wooden points. Adrian made pitch by boiling down pine sap to remove the water. When it was boiling he added a few pinches of hardwood ash as a thickener. When it was done he used the pitch combined with small tendons to fasten flint tips to the darts. In two days, he was ready.

He had fully penetrated the mountains. They were everything he had expected and hoped for—and more. The cool air carried soft scents of pines and flowers. Everything was still green except the hardwoods—they had started turning and the colors were spectacular. He traveled deeper into the mountains every day, not knowing when or where he would stop for the winter. But he would stop when he found the right place.

During his trip he had avoided people and any sign of civilization by giving them a wide berth. This had slowed his trip considerably, but after encountering the folks in the canyon he knew he was not fit company for others, and felt no desire to be around people. However, his curiosity was piqued when he came across the signs of a village deep in the mountains. He worked his way into a position to watch. He saw a well-organized village of about sixty people. Four days he watched them; they were a curiosity. They had a good farming system using mules and horses. He also noticed that the village put out sentries and hid their livestock deep in the woods at the first sign of anyone approaching.

The homes were all of log construction. There was no sign that there had ever been electricity in the village, no wires or poles of any kind could be seen in the little valley. The road leading through the village was gravel, an all-weather road, but he saw no cars or trucks of any kind, and no garages either. After two days he was convinced that these people had adopted an 1800s lifestyle before the grid went down. They could have been Amish, except they didn't dress Amish. They dressed in normal, modern clothes. The village was a busy place with two stores that apparently took in trade, selling and buying by barter. It had a blacksmith shop, a small tannery, and a gristmill on the banks of a nearby stream.

Apparently they had been little affected by the grid dropping, having their means of livelihood already worked out in advance. They were not reliant on electricity or outside trade. By some quirk of fate, and their remote location and distance from cities, they had survived well. He silently wished them continued good luck as he traveled on.

He didn't travel much further, only about twenty miles. He found himself in a remote valley with a good stream running through it. The weather had begun to turn cold and nasty. It had snowed a little the previous day, and he knew it was time to set up a winter camp. He scouted the valley and found no signs of people. There were elk and black bears roaming the area. The stream had fish in it. Everything he needed was right here, especially solitude. He began to settle in.

CHAPTER 7

ADRIAN THRUST THE SPEAR INTO the bear's open mouth, cutting its tongue badly. The bear roared and flung its head from side to side at the stinging pain, then charged again, furiously snapping its jaws like huge steel traps, and swinging at him with long, sharp claws. Adrian backed up carefully, ducking and dodging, continually stabbing the spear at the bear's nose and face.

He had been startled to find a grizzly bear in these mountains this time of year; most bears were in hibernation. The bear had looked at Adrian as though he were food, and Adrian had instantly seen the bear as a life or death challenge. They both refused to back down from this fight to the death. Almost on first sight, they charged at each other. Adrian was armed with a flint-tipped spear. It was a tiny weapon against the two thousand pound bear, but Adrian wasn't concerned with losing. If he lost, he lost. That was all there was to it. He'd had no intention of losing, but was well aware that he could.

Adrian felt the back of his thighs press against a large fallen log. He was pinned. He couldn't back up any farther without taking the time to climb over the log, and that would be all the opening the bear needed to finish Adrian off.

He kept prodding at the bear with the spear. The cut tongue had given the bear a small measure of respect for this little animal it was intent on eating. Adrian lunged at an opening after ducking another huge paw swiping at his head. He had an open shot at the bear's head and lunged in with the spear, hitting the bear squarely in its left eye.

The bear roared and backed up, pawing at its head, trying to understand the stinging pain and darkness that had suddenly over took the left side of his field of vision. Adrian took full advantage of the bear's partial blindness by circling around it, staying within the bear's new blind spot. He had opening after opening now to attack, and lunged and stabbed with the spear each time. He was wounding the bear, wounds that might eventually bring it down, but if they did it wouldn't be during this fight. Adrian kept circling, stabbing the bear, but the shallow wounds served more to enrage it than to hinder it. He was counting on that rage to cause it to make a mistake, and it did.

The bear tried to whirl rapidly to get Adrian in sight again, but tangled its legs and fell heavily. Adrian rushed in and drove the spear as deep into the bear's chest throwing his full weight onto the spear. He felt the flint point scrape between ribs, and then suddenly it was past the muscle and bone resistance and plunged deep into the chest. The bear would die now, and soon. Adrian backed off and stood ready to run if necessary. The bear, mortally wounded, snapped and bit at the spear shaft protruding from its chest. It moved slower and slower as the wounded heart pumped blood into the chest cavity. Adrian watched as the bear roared for the last time, king of the mountains no more, then lay down, twitched, and became still.

Now t was time to tend to his own wounds. He had been badly slashed by the bear's claws. They cuts would be filthy from the claws and become infected if not cleaned and patched up immediately. Shaking from the adrenalin still flooding into his bloodstream, but now with no physical outlet, he pulled the remainder of his shirt off and inspected the slashes. There were four of them, deep and long. Before the grid went down he would have been given antibiotics and about a hundred stitches. The best he could do now would be to clean the wounds. As he looked around for a creek he noticed that the bear had been trying to knock down a large tree.

Curious as to why, Adrian studied the tree for a moment. He saw a hole in the trunk about halfway up. Adrian thought perhaps a colony of bees had made their nest within it. Maybe the bear had smelled honey and was trying to get at it when Adrian surprised him. Honey was good news, if he could find a way to reach it. Honey was a good wound preserver. Coating a wound with honey not only kept it clean, but honey had natural antibiotic properties. This was why honey could be stored forever without ever going bad. He climbed the tree and found he could reach the hole. Although he knew it was risky to reach into a place he couldn't see, he did and came out with a piece of honeycomb grasped in his hand. About a dozen bees came with it, stinging him all over. They hurt like blazes!

Dropping to the ground, he put the honeycomb into his shirt to keep it clean, climbed back up, and came back with more honey. Once more he went up and came down. He wanted enough honey to put on the wounds every day until they healed over, and he wouldn't be talking himself into climbing up and getting stung like this again, not after the wounds stiffened up. To soothe the bee stings he used a finger nail to scrape out the stingers and then coated the spots with the raw honey. Honey, he knew, contained enzymes that counteracted the stingers venom and stopped the pain within five minutes. With the honey wrapped in his shirt, he walked back to his camp. He needed to boil water to clean the wounds. After that he would skin the bear and butcher it. With the freezing weather he had time, the meat wouldn't spoil.

He had set up a winter camp by building a wickiup—a simple structure built by burying the ends of saplings in a circle then bending their tops over and tying them together. Once they were tied together, smaller poles were woven in between the bent poles, and then smaller ones until a dense mat had been formed. At that stage it looked like a large, upside down basket. This he then covered with pine boughs laid on the skeleton in a circle from the bottom up, shingle style, the better to shed water. He wove brush and grass bundles in until there was a dense covering of material over the entire framework, then forced a small slit in one spot as the entry.

It served as a good windbreak, and was fairly dry in a light rain. He had tanned the hides of elk and deer he had killed, and sewn them together with overlapping edges. After greasing them with fat, he laid them over the top of the brush on the wickiup. Once covered with hides it was rain proof. A small hole in the roof let out smoke from the fire that he kept inside. Fire had to be carefully controlled or the thing could go up in a blaze with him in it. To prevent a spark from causing the wickiup to go up in flames, he gathered clay from the creek and plastered the inside framework with a coating of clay mixed with dry grasses. This also kept the inside air trapped in place, creating a warm, dry shelter. It had been easy to make—a few of days of labor plus the time to get the skins. It wouldn't last long, but it would last the winter, and that was enough. The clay coating required almost daily maintenance, but that was a small chore.

Carrying on with the Stone Age lifestyle, he made a cooking pot out of deer hide. He tanned it, removed the fur, and then tied it to a hoop rim he had made. When filled with water it could be suspended over a fire and the water inside prevented the hide from burning, even as the water boiled. As long as the flames stayed below the waterline it worked. It was difficult to keep clean and sanitary, but it made excellent stews. He carefully washed it out after each use, and then refilled it with water, which he boiled to sterilize it. He also dug a pit that the hide fit into, then put fire-heated rocks in the stew to boil it. This had the advantage of leaking less, but also required constant changing of the heated rocks. He had learned not to use rocks from the creek; they contained water and sometimes exploded in the fire as they heated.

Adrian had built an underground oven for cooking small game quickly, smaller but similar to the ones used to cook the Sotol plants in the Palo Duro canyon. It was a quick and efficient method of cooking. He had made a wooden bowl by burning out the center of a burl with hot coals and scraping. It was the work of one evening and made eating easier, especially stew. His wooden bowl and spoon were thoroughly washed after each use and sterilized with boiling water. Sanitation was paramount to survival.

Lye soap was easy to make and a great boon to sanitation. Water leached through hardwood ashes picked up the lye. This solution was then boiled down to concentrate the lye. Elk tallow was melted and mixed with the lye solution, then the whole thing was left to set and harden for a few days.

In good weather he sat by a fire outside until he was sleepy. Sometimes he would play the harmonica after dark. He played blues style, riffing up and down, crossing over the notes to create melodies that came close to expressing his grief. The music helped and at the same time hurt, just as it had when he had lost his parents. He could express his feelings out loud with this music in a way he never could otherwise. He had played often for Alice after she gave it to him, happier music to be sure, but once in a while something like these. Alice had loved his music. At times he hoped she could somehow hear him playing now, but he didn't really believe it.

When he got back to his wickiup, he boiled water. He didn't have a needle or thread fine enough to stitch the wounds, but he did have an old shirt that he could use for bandages. He cleaned the wounds with the water after it boiled, then soaked the shirt in boiling water. While the shirt was soaking he used some of the honey to saturate the wounds, covering them with as much honey as possible. When the shirt was clean he tore it into strips and wrapped them around his arm and chest as best he could. He rewrapped the surplus honey, took it two-hundred yards from his camp and stored it in suspending it on a cord as high as he could reach on a tree limb. He didn't want the smell of honey to draw a bear to his wickiup.

Having accomplished these chores, it was time to skin the bear. The real work was about to start. Adrian had killed a black bear in the fall, and found the eating superb. The fat was especially good and packed a load of calories. This bear was too big to eat unless it was preserved. With the winter's cold to keep the meat from spoiling he had time to make it into pemmican, his favored trail food.

It took Adrian two days to skin and butcher the bear completely. It took him a week to cut and hang the meat on drying racks. In the meantime, he feasted on bear steak dripping with fat three times a day. He used the bear's brains to tan the hide; it would make an excellent robe for the winter. He rendered the fat from the meat before drying it, and extracted the marrow from the bones. When the meat was as dry as he could get it, he pulverized it between two rocks. The lard was heated and the pulverized meat mixed in until a thick paste was achieved. This was then pressed into sewn skin bags while the concoction was hot. When it cooled it hardened. It would be softer in warmer weather, but it would remain good for years if kept cool and dry. A man could get fat eating pemmican.

By the time Adrian had prepared the bear meat, a week had gone by and he was sick and feverish from the wounds. The honey had helped, but the wounds still showed signs of infection. Adrian had twice boiled water and treated the wounds with the boiling water, trying to get the poison out, then covering them again with honey. It was a tedious and painful procedure. Adrian slept a lot while healing. He had fever dreams about Alice. He was half delirious and believed that she was with him in the wickiup. When he awoke each morning he was forced to learn all over again that she was gone.

Adrian's grief had not abated. He didn't think it had gotten any better either; it seemed to him that each new day he had sunk deeper into hell. He recalled Roman's warnings, and knew them to be true. Adrian hadn't reached the part Roman had predicted, where the pain would level off. When he had first gotten to the mountains that fall he had spotted and bypassed three small tribes and the village. He had discovered in the Palo Duro that being around people intensified the pain. He had no interest in people. He wanted nothing to do with them.

Adrian went to sleep on the eighth night after the bear fight. He was sick, his wounds were infected, and he had a high fever. He didn't know it, but he would nearly die within the next twenty-four hours, and would soon be dealing with people again, whether he wanted to or not.

CHAPTER 8

ADRIAN AWOKE THE NEXT MORNING with a high fever. He needed water to treat the wounds again. He staggered when he tried to get up. He grabbed his spear to use as a walking stick to steady himself. The sky carried omens of a blizzard. The clouds were thick, dark gray, and low. Wind blew out of the North. Adrian, in a semi-delirious state, didn't notice these ominous signs. His fever made it seem warmer than it was. He left the wickiup in buckskin pants, shirt, and moccasins, leaning on his spear, carrying the hide kettle to fetch water. He left the bearskin robe in the wickiup, stumbling frequently as he walked. He didn't take his handmade snowshoes with him as he normally did.

When he stooped to get water he became extremely dizzy. He sat down, then passed out. When he came to he didn't know where he was. He was in a full fever delirium, and couldn't remember that he had gone to the creek for water. He didn't recognize the creek or any of the familiar landmarks near his camp. Struggling to walk he used the spear to lean on. He crossed the creek and began moving further and further away from camp. He had not noticed the hide kettle, and left it where it dropped.

Snow had started falling and the temperature was dropping rapidly. Instinctively he was following an elk trail through the forest. He was looking for shelter; he knew he needed shelter. In spite of his spiking fever, he had become bitterly cold. The cold was slowing his thinking, and the fever was distorting it. After two hours of halting travel he could go no further. He found a large tree and sat against it, on the downwind side. It made a poor windbreak. Adrian began to lose consciousness. He dreamt of Alice, convinced she was with him. Adrian was dying rapidly from exposure, but there was a trace of a smile on his face. He hadn't been so happy since before Alice died.

While Adrian was stumbling away from his camp, Marian and her son were walking along a cross trail. They had been away from their cabin all day, hunting for game. They had not killed anything. Despite being so near to starvation, Marian still recognized the storm that was coming and had headed for home. Her cabin was six miles across rugged terrain from Adrian's camp. Neither of them were aware of the other's existence. Marian's husband had died months earlier. She hoped to make it through the winter, then find a village or tribe that would take them in. Jerod was seven years old and weak with hunger.

They were miles from the cabin and quickly losing the trail under the deepening snow. Marian had decided to begin looking for temporary shelter from the storm when she literally stumbled over Adrian. He had fallen sideways onto the ground and was almost as pale as the ground he lay on. Snow was sticking to his hair and beard and clothing. Marian was shocked to find him. She checked his throat for a pulse. His skin was ice cold, but there was a faint beating in his neck.

"Jerod, fetch wood—quickly!" They gathered fire wood and she built three fires in a triangle in front of the tree and Adrian. She left only enough room inside the fires for the three of them to huddle. They were going to get wet, but if they could keep the fires going they could stay warm enough to survive, if not comfortably. The fires would also help to warm Adrian. She and Jerod propped Adrian up and they sat on each side of him, making as much contact as possible to share their body heat. It got dark early because of the storm. It would be a long night.

Adrian's fever had peaked. Had he still been in the wickiup, he would have recovered nicely. The hypothermia that had come on brought him to the edge of death. Adrian knew in a distant way that he was dying, and was satisfied to go. The pain was ending and would soon be gone. Yet something deep in Adrian resisted death. Dying without fighting back wasn't in his makeup. He would have died anyway had it not been for Marian and Jerod and the fires. Warmth started to slowly creep back into his extremities and then into his body core. He had small areas of frost bite on his hands and feet.

Adrian fought a long, slow battle that lasted the entire night and well into the next morning. He didn't regain consciousness until Marian and the boy were dead. When he awoke, he was angry. The part of him that fought to live was deep within his psyche, something he wasn't aware of. What he was aware of was that he had almost escaped the strangling grief. But he had been rudely snatched back. He opened his eyes to see what had gone wrong. Near him lay a dead child. He saw two brutish men, crudely dressed. One of them was pulling up his pants. At his feet lay a dead woman with her skirt rucked up above her waist.

He saw three fires smoldering around him. The picture was instantly clear, partly because his subconscious mind had been gathering information while he was unconscious—but mostly because the situation was self-evident. Obviously the men had seen Adrian as no threat in his weakened and unconscious condition and probably intended to interrogate him after they raped the woman.

Adrian's anger at being alive was compounded a hundred times by what these men had done, and by the fact that he had lain there unaware while they did it. Roaring like the grizzly bear he had so recently vanquished, he grabbed his spear and thrust it directly into the throat of the man pulling his pants up. He pulled it out as blood jetted from the man's carotid artery in red, arcing sprays, then shoved it deep into the man's stomach. The man tried to scream but could only make gurgling sounds as he sank to his knees in the reddening snow, clutching at the spear with both hands.

Without pausing, and still roaring, Adrian grabbed the other man, who had barely moved in his shock at this sudden ferocious attack and his companion's blood raining over him. Adrian seized the man by the throat and choked him with hands of iron fury. Adrian put his face inches from the dying man's as he choked him and screamed with inarticulate rage. Adrian kept choking and screaming until the man was dead, his lounge protruding from his mouth from being strangled. Then Adrian slowly released his grip.

The snow had stopped during the night and the fires had partially dried Adrian off. His fever was gone, but he was weak from the long sickness and the sudden activity.

He was trembling with adrenalin as he surveyed the grisly sight before him. The two men he had killed. The woman, her throat cut. The boy with a smashed in skull. Adrian, now beyond sanity, stared without compassion, only intense anger. Who were these people to have brought him back to this wretched life; brought him back to this mess? Adrian didn't know where he was. He was lost, and the sun was behind clouds, so he couldn't determine directions.

He could see that he was at a crossing of two elk trails, so he had six choices. Follow one of the four trails, strike out cross country off the trails, or stay where he was. He chose to follow one of the trails. Before he set out, he searched the four bodies for anything useful. The men had rifles, poor ones, and a small amount of ammo for each. One of them had matches. He left the rifles but took the coat off the man he strangled—the other one was too bloody. He chose the trail that headed downhill. It would eventually lead him to water, and he was ravenously thirsty and hungry. He could catch fish and eat. Taking his spear from the dead man's stomach, he moved down the trail.

He reached a creek after a couple of hours. At the creek he saw where wood had been chopped. That meant that someone had a camp nearby. He needed to check that out before doing anything else. He drank water, cold water that lowered his internal temperature again. He felt the weakness increasing with the cold. Carefully scouting the area, he found a well-established trail from the creek up the other bank. He followed it by walking parallel to it. It led to a small cabin that looked well-made and tight. There was no smoke from the short stone chimney. He circled around the cabin but all signs said it was empty.

He found a grave nearby. By the looks of the marker it was only a few months old.

Adrian approached the cabin and knocked on the hewn plank door, yelling out as he did. "Anyone home?" Twice more he knocked, then opened the door and stepped into the dark one-room cabin. There were no windows; the only light came in through the open door behind him. It was neat and clean. The occupants had not been gone long. An old photo on the mantle told him the woman had lived here, with a man, most likely her husband and the boy's father. Adrian assumed the man was buried in the grave.

Using the firewood and kindling that was ready at hand, he quickly built a fire in the neatly made fireplace. He was cold and half-starved. There was no food. He had pemmican back at his camp, lots of it. All he had to do was find it. When he did he would bring it here. This cabin was too good to leave behind for the wickiup, and the owners were all dead. He sat at the table, letting the heat from the fire soak into him. He thought about where he had awoken and decided that he had a fair idea of which way his camp was. Instead of going back to the three fires camp, he would cut across country, taking the third leg of the triangle.

After he had traveled several miles in what he felt was the right direction he recognized a lightning struck tree, and all at once the location of his camp clicked into place. The cabin was two valleys over from his. It was only a matter of hours before he was back at the wickiup, sitting by his fire and wolfing down bear pemmican. He stayed there two more days, recovering his strength. Then he moved all his supplies to the cabin. He hid his food high up in several trees. He might lose some of it to accident or animal, but he wasn't going to lose all of it. He had more than enough pemmican to take him well into spring.

When Adrian had been in the new cabin for two days he went to get the woman's and child's bodies. It nagged at him that they had done what they thought was a good deed, saving his life—they hadn't known better. He couldn't repay that by leaving them to the forest scavengers. Insane as he now was, there was still a tiny thread of something civilized deep inside. Cursing himself for being seven kinds of a fool, he took an elk hide and walked back to the death camp. Everything was as he had left it except the bodies were frozen solid. It made carrying them difficult. He built a travois using poles and the hide, put the bodies and the rifles and ammo on it, and dragged them back to the cabin. Using their shovel he dug two new graves next to the older one. He buried them, thought about if he should say something, but decided there was no point talking to himself. He buried them in silence. He lived in silence and misery for three more days before the silence was broken, and Adrian's war started.

CHAPTER 9

T HE SILENCE ADRIAN LIVED IN existed not only externally, but also inside his head. He rarely thought in words now. His thinking was as acute as before, but faster without words to slow him down. Words created imprecise images; thinking without words was simpler and more effective when alone. He went about his daily chores with complete awareness of his surroundings. He heard every sound, saw every movement. He spotted patterns in the trees and brush that he would never have noticed before. He smelled things clearly, especially when he hadn't been around his fire for a few hours. His senses were fully attuned to his environment in a way that he had never experienced in his life. Only the pain of grief kept him from being a contented man.

He listened far better than ever before. Sudden silences meant something to him now. The forest was awash with the sounds of birds and wildlife coming from all directions. A silence in one part of the forest meant something was moving there, something the birds and squirrels were afraid of. Usually a predator of one kind or another. It might be an eagle or a bear or a wolf. Once he had spotted a mountain lion by the circle of silence it created around it as it prowled. He had tracked it down and killed it with his bow. Mountain men of old had often said it was the best eating in the mountains, and Adrian agreed.

Knowing that he, too, was a predator, he took extra care not to disturb the forest life around him, and as a result he had become a more efficient hunter. When he hunted he covered himself with an elk skin that still had the head on it. Moving along the way an elk does he not only blended in, but was able to keep the birds singing. It was an old Indian trick he had read about, and it was effective. The skin also allowed him to stalk elk and deer much closer than before. They saw him as another safe animal grazing along. In one instance a bull elk had come towards him to investigate what appeared to be a lone cow that could be added to its herd. When he finally realized what the bull was after, an alarmed Adrian urgently threw the skin off and stood upright, yelling and waving his arms. The bull nearly turned itself inside out trying to spin and run away. The whole situation was so comical that Adrian burst into rare laughter.

Adrian also used a small, stuffed deerskin dummy to attract deer. He would set it on the edge of a clearing and climb a nearby tree. Using grass reeds held between his thumbs and blowing air across it, he could make a good imitation of a fawn's distress cry. Deer would hear and come investigate, see the decoy, and approach. Predators would too. It was a deadly technique and brought him much food.

He had taken the cabin over, admiring the skill and craftsmanship with which it had been built. The man who built it was a good man; that was evident in everything about the place. He could read the man's character by his work and the care he took in crafting; it was plain to anyone that could see. It had not been built quickly or crudely, but with loving skill in every notch in every timber. The timbers had been shaped top and bottom to fit tightly against each other. There was no chinking, yet no air came through, no daylight showed. Adrian was sure this meant that the logs were tongue and grooved into each other. A small piece of cast-off timber he found later had proved it.

The door was built with wooden hinges, one piece with a hole and one with a peg fit into the hole, lightly greased. Most cabin doors were attached with strips of leather for hinges, but these were carefully carved wood. The door moved smoothly and silently on them, always keeping the door in perfect alignment. It had a similarly carved latch that could be opened from the outside or locked when inside. There were eating bowls, plates, forks, and spoons also beautifully carved of wood. He found two combs intricately carved of turtle shell that were quite effective. The stones making the fireplace weren't just stacked; whoever had made it had used colorful stones to make a sunrise pattern. This man had been an artist, showing his love of creating in everything he touched. Adrian would have liked to have known him.

He had been in the cabin a little over a week when he sensed someone watching him. He was alerted to the presence by the unnatural cone of silence nearby. He was walking to the cabin with firewood in both hands when he heard the rushing footsteps of two men behind him. "Crap," he thought, "they sound like elephants, do they really think I don't hear that?" He knew that they wanted to capture him, otherwise they would have shot at him from their hiding place. Adrian smiled grimly and kept walking towards the cabin. He could tell that the two men were separated by about ten feet between them by the sounds they were making. The one to Adrian's left was the bigger man, at least thirty pounds heavier than his companion and faster too. He would be the one to take out first.

Adrian stopped and shifted the bundle of wood in his arms, as though adjusting the load. He timed it so that as the two men were about to pounce he dropped the wood; except for one piece that he used as a club. He whirled to his left, swinging the club at where he knew the man's head would be. He swung through, and the heavy wood moving at full of speed crushed the man's skull like a ripe watermelon. Blood and brains sprayed out in gray and crimson lace. The man was instantly dead; his body fell skidding past Adrian before grinding to a halt in the snow.

Adrian continued swinging even as the man's body hit the ground, turning completely around to face the other man. Adrian saw shock on the man's face. He was trying to stop but his speed carried him right into Adrian's arms. Adrian flipped the man over his hip, using his momentum against him. The man hit the ground heavily, his breath knocked out of him. Adrian kicked him in the temple hard enough to knock him out. Adrian had some questions for him. He grimly welcomed the interruption by the two men; it gave him something interesting to do.

Adrian glanced once at the heavier man and confirmed he was dead. No man survived a head flattened that much. He grabbed the other man by the collar and dragged him to the cabin wall. He propped the man in a sitting position against the wall, then fetched a hammer and nails. He nailed the man's hands to the wall, arms outstretched. Secure in the knowledge that this fellow wasn't going anywhere, he dragged the dead body and propped it in a sitting position next to his prisoner, something for him to look at and consider. Adrian picked up the fallen firewood and finished his chores. He heated stew and ate a hot meal. As he was finishing he heard stirring sounds coming from his prisoner.

"Perfect timing," he thought to himself, using words again. "Must be a consequence of being around people, and the fact that I will be speaking in a minute." Adrian took one of the hand-crafted chairs outside and sat in front of his prisoner. He stayed just out of reach of the man's feet, in case he was feeling frisky and wanted to kick. He waited patiently, allowing the man to regain consciousness at his own pace. Adrian was in no hurry. The man slowly came to, opening and closing his eyes several times, each time seeming a little more aware. Finally, the man, fully awake, tried to move his hands and grunted in pain as he felt the nails and realized what had been done to him. The terror on his face pleased Adrian.

"So, you come sneaking up behind me, try to take me prisoner," said Adrian. "Then you go to sleep. Then you wake up, nailed to a wall, a prisoner. I betcha you're thinking about begging for mercy, right? If I asked you how you were going to treat me as your prisoner, you would tell me you were going to treat me nice. Shoot, you probably have ice cream and cake back there where you left your rifles, just for me, right? So now that I have done your lying for you, let me tell you what's going to happen.

"You're going to answer all of my questions. You're going to answer them honestly and completely. You're going to tell me anything interesting or important that I don't ask you about. In short, you're about to talk, a lot, because if you don't I am going to bring pain to you that you never knew existed. You'll be begging me to kill you, but I won't do it. And eventually you'll tell me everything that I want to know anyway. Now, think about that until I get back, then decide how this is going to be for you. Your choice entirely, I have all the time in the world and nothing better to do."

Adrian rose from his chair and looked down at the prisoner. He turned and walked off to examine the tracks the two men had left in the snow. He walked to where they had hidden and watched. Their rifles were leaning against a tree. He followed their tracks a few yards back into the woods making sure there were only the two, then returned to gather up their rifles. He carried them past the prisoner into the cabin. One of the rifles was an excellent long range shooter with a top of the line scope on it. He came back out and searched the dead man and found fifty rounds of ammo for the rifle. It was a true treasure. This re-affirmed his notion that they had wanted him alive, and the only reason could be for questioning, possibly about the two dead men back at the three fires camp.

He took the ammo inside and got his huge bowie knife down from the mantle. He took out the whetstone also. He returned outside and sat in the chair. Adrian began slowly and deliberately honing the already surgically sharp knife. Adrian knew that he rhythmic sound of the whetstone on the knife blade would badly rasp on the prisoner's frayed nerves. From the looks of his hands, he had barely tried to get free when Adrian was out of sight. This told Adrian the man would talk freely because his pain tolerance was low. If Adrian had been nailed to the wall, he would have ripped his hands off those nails no matter how much it hurt or how much damage was incurred. He would then beat his captor to death with those bloody wounded hands. This man had just sat there. He would talk.

Adrian waited, stroking the knife on the stone. Suddenly the man started blabbering, stuttering because he was trying to talk so fast.

"I c-come from Wolfgang's c-camp. It's eight or ten miles northwest of here at an old mining site. We were in prison when the grid went down. The prison near Lyons. The doors were supposed to stay in lockdown when the power was off, so we were going to starve. But something went wrong in the system and some of the doors opened up. Wolfgang's cell was one of them. He got out and figured out how to work the rest of the doors open. He released everyone except the enemies he had in there, and he had a lot of enemies. They starved; we checked later. The rest he told to go away, or to follow him, he didn't care which. But, he said, 'If you follow me, you take my orders without question or hesitation. I don't have time to babysit. You don't want to take my orders, don't follow me. You follow me and don't take my orders—I'll kill you.' It was easy to see he meant it. Like most of the guys, I had nowhere to go, no idea what to do. He looked like he had a plan, that kind of guy always knows what to do next, and is good at it. So I followed him. I took his orders, and he did us good. We almost always have food, and places to sleep.

"We raided everything in the town worth raiding. When the town dried up, we moved to the woods. We raided homes and camps. We eventually found and settled in the mining camp. It's a good location with a small river for water, cabins to sleep in. There are tribes and villages in the area that we make give us food. We hunt some too; we have a couple of pretty good hunters that bring in elk now and then.

"Me and Lynn were sent out to see what happened to the scouts that didn't come back. We found their bodies, found tracks leading here. We watched you for a few minutes an decided that cause you were alone and unarmed we'd rush in an grab you before you knew what was up. Then we was gonna find out what you did to our men. We was gonna take you back an let Wolfgang decide what to do with you. We figured he'd torture you for a few days then kill you when he got bored. It's what he usually does."

Adrian waited, but the prisoner seemed to have run down. "How many men are there?"

"Seventy two, including Wolfgang himself."

"All from that prison break?"

"Sure, well mostly. We picked up some here and there."

"How are they armed?"

"Rifles and pistols. What we could find in sporting goods stores or take from people. Nothing like military stuff, more like hunting stuff."

"How long you been at the mining camp?"

"Since winter started," the prisoner said.

Adrian sat and thought awhile. "Tell you what I'm going to do. I'm going to turn you loose to go back to Wolfgang and give him a message for me. You tell him that he started this war, and that I'm happy to oblige him. You tell him to get ready. Tell him Adrian Hunter will be along directly."

CHAPTER 10

ADRIAN RELEASED HIS PRISONER AND gave him a brief head start. He packed pemmican and his bow and arrows and his flint knife. Adrian thought, "Just to make it interesting, I'll bring them a Stone Age war." Adrian was thinking of this as a sporting event, a deadly game, but a game nonetheless. His rage at these men was unabated. The rage helped to keep the pain at bay, the insanity helped to keep him from finding the pain, and this war would be the ultimate diversion.

He followed the ex-prisoner to the mining camp. Adrian suspected that the ex-prisoner was already a dead man. He figured that Wolfgang, from the description he had been given, would be embarrassed to have lost three men, and then to have this wounded and therefore useless mouth to feed show up ·and announce a war—that would pretty much be a kill the messenger situation. Double up on that; Wolfgang would realize that his man had talked freely to the enemy and his death was not only a sure bet, but it would be slow and painful. It would be a warning to the other men, and help wash away the stain of embarrassment.

Adrian watched from the woods as the ex-prisoner disappeared into the largest of the cabins, obviously Wolfgang's. He then scouted around the camp's fringes, locating and noting vantage points. The mining camp was in a bowl-shaped depression surrounded by woods. There was clear space all around the cabins for two hundred yards. No trees, just short brush. It was easy to spy on the place, dozens of good hiding spots all around it. Adrian saw the main cabin and ten slightly smaller cabins. Across the river there was a long, open-sided structure—a pavilion filled with picnic tables that must serve as the eating and gathering place. The river was small, closer to a creek in size. There was a footbridge across it leading to the pavilion.

It was an excellent set up for Wolfgang, or had been up to now. "Now," Adrian thought, "it's their death trap. They couldn't have chosen a better spot for me to destroy them. Beautiful." Adrian continued to take note of the camp's layout. There were four main trails that led out of the camp. One was the mining camp road where truck traffic had obviously come and gone in the mining days. There were three wide paths worn smooth by foot traffic. Obviously these men were creatures of habit, and felt no threats from their victims. Otherwise they wouldn't have such obvious trails. They were going to make this easy, at first. As they learned they would become harder to get at, but it should be an easy ride for a while.

Adrian settled in to watch the camp until dark. It wasn't long before the ex-prisoner was dragged out of Wolfgang's cabin by four men; he was kicking and screaming—he knew what was going to happen. They tied him to one of the corner posts on the picnic building. Then a man dressed in a wolf skin coat came out, obviously Wolfgang.

The wolf skin coat told Adrian a lot about the man's ego. Wolfgang began cutting the ex-prisoner with a knife. His screams were easily heard by Adrian. It lasted a long time.

What happened later shocked Adrian, a feeling that had become very unfamiliar in the past few months. As soon as the man was dead, he was skinned and butchered like a pig. A large fire was built in a spot that had been obviously used many times before for the purpose. The butchered man's remains were roasted over the fire on a wrought iron rotisserie, turned by hand. The meat was just barely cooked through when the men began tearing into it with a frenzy. As darkness gathered, Adrian watched a scene out of a nightmare; men moving around the fire, roaring with laughter as they ate their former comrade. Adrian had encountered signs of cannibalism after the grid went down. It wasn't at all uncommon. But he had never actually witnessed it being performed. He considered the creatures before him no longer as men. Now they were disgusting cretins, beasts that must be killed. This would now be a war of total extermination, a slow war of attrition, but one of annihilation. He would continue with the primitive weapons and techniques, and he would be in it to the end.

Roman had once told Adrian that psychopaths were perhaps the best at survival in any situation. "They don't have an ounce of empathy in them," he had said. "They'll do whatever it takes to survive and do it without a second's hesitation. They will climb over anyone. They're smart, quick to act, and completely centered on their own needs and wants. Psychopaths have a different brain structure from normal people. They are in effect animals in human skin. They normally number about one percent of the population, so there were an estimated three-million of them before the grid dropped. But now, given their natural survival abilities, most of those three-million will have survived and mixed into the much reduced population… making up perhaps as much as twenty percent.

"They will tend to become leaders of gangs because they are skilled at using other people and they thrive on power. Gangs will increase their effectiveness at getting what they want. They are master manipulators. I read an article that claimed many corporate CEOs were psychopaths; they naturally gravitated to the top because they had no morals and would do whatever it took. Lying, cheating, stealing, manipulating, anything at all. They destroy their rivals' careers with impunity because their rivals play by the rules of society, and psychopaths fight by the rule of consequences only. They acknowledge no other rules. Learn the signs and if you run across any of them, whatever else you do, don't trust them and don't hesitate to take whatever action is necessary. They won't."

Adrian knew he was watching a psychopath. Adrian doubted his real name was Wolfgang; more likely it was part of his manipulative techniques. He had all of the hallmarks that Roman had warned him about.

When darkness fell completely Adrian went back to the cabin. Adrian thought, "Sure as God made little green apples, he'll send men here in the morning with orders to bring me back alive at all costs. He wants to nip this embarrassment in the bud." He removed all of his possessions and hid them in the forest. Armed with his spear, bow and flint knife he camped away from the cabin. By fire light he removed his arrows from their quiver and modified them.

He removed the stone tips from the arrows, sharpened the ends to pinpoints, then carefully cut into the wood toward the point, near the tip. This created barbs of splinter wood on each arrow. He cut a deep ring completely around the shaft three inches down from the point. He dipped the arrow tips into bear dung that he gathered for the purpose. He would soak the wood in the dung overnight. When a man was shot with one of these, he would not be in immediate danger of death, unless a major artery or organ was hit. But he would die, eventually and slowly from infection. He cut the barbs into the arrows so that when it was pulled out the contaminated splinters would break off in the wound and remain. With a little luck the entire head would break off at the weak place he created by cutting the ring around the shaft.

Only a skilled doctor with a sterile surgical suite and antibiotics could save a man shot with one of these. Wolfgang would soon have a bunch of wounded men on his hands.

"It'll be a dilemma for Wolfgang," Adrian thought to himself. "He can't start killing and eating all of his wounded; the rest of the men will desert him if he does. He has to try and save them. They'll get extremely sick and will be in excruciating pain. This will dishearten the healthy men; terrorize them with thoughts of being in that condition too. Wolfgang will not only have this demoralizing force in his camp, but he'll have to dedicate manpower and resources to aid them. For every five or six wounded men, screaming in agony and dying slow terrifying deaths, there'll be at least one healthy man taken out of action to care for them. Beautiful, just plain beautiful." Adrian slept well that night.

Before daylight the next morning he had chosen his ambush spot. He was certain that the hunting party would come in as straight a line as they could, and that the ex-prisoner had told them exactly where to go. Adrian set up at a point halfway to the cabin. His first ambush spot was the top of a short cliff they would pass by. It gave him an easy field of fire. His plan was to ambush them at several points. His goal was to send everyone back wounded with the slow death arrows. It depended on how many men were sent. He would make more poisoned arrows later; they were easy enough to make. But for now, he had fourteen to work with.

Shortly after daylight, they came. There were eight of them. "Excellent," Adrian thought. "I have more than enough arrows. Eight will be a treat to send back. Wolfgang won't understand at first why they were wounded in such a minor way. He'll think he is up against some kind of stealthy but ineffective idiot. Later, he'll realize the true nature of the attack, and will be spitting mad."

The men were walking single-file. Adrian waited until the last man passed by, stood, and fired three arrows in quick succession. Each arrow hit one of the men in the lower back or thigh. The other men, slow to react because of the silence of the attack, began shooting in all directions. Adrian had taken cover long before they began to shoot, and they had not seen him so they didn't know where to aim. It was all Adrian could do not to laugh.

Before they had finished shooting Adrian was on his way to the next ambush spot. He thought he could probably get two more next time. They would certainly be more alert and react faster. Adrian thought, "If they continue on to the cabin they make themselves vulnerable. There are hundreds of places I can hide and shoot one at a time. If they go back to camp I can do the same thing. They don't understand what they're up against."

Half an hour later the men appeared, still in single-file. The three Adrian had wounded weren't with them. They had either been sent back to camp or told to wait until the unit returned. Adrian's guess was they were told to return to camp. They had set out a point man, in this case the safest position in the line. They had not set out flankers, Adrian wished they would. It would be so simple to pick those men off.

Again, Adrian waited for the men to pass by, stood, and released two arrows. He watched the two arrows sink deep into the muscle tissue of the two men. Adrian retreated and moved to the next spot, listening to the sound of panicked gun fire behind him. His long bow was a powerful weapon. Made from the seasoned Bois D'Arc, he had carefully shaped it to be as strong as he could pull. He had backed it with elk tendon and hide glue, then wrapped it in wet rawhide that was tightly sewn together. When the rawhide dried, it pulled tight, making a compression sleeve that along with the tendons increased the strength of the bow, and protected the wood from splintering. The string was made of braided elk tendon. Adrian shot it Indian style, pinching the arrow nock with thumb and forefinger, making for a fast, smooth release. The bow had elk horn tips to hold the string.

Three men were left uninjured. The trick now was to guess whether they would continue forward or return to camp. Adrian was betting on the men continuing forward. They would have pulled out the wooden arrows and thought them relatively harmless, only having sharp points and no broad-heads to do a lot of cutting. They would also be scared of Wolfgang's reaction. "Afraid to be called cowards. Afraid of being served as dinner," he thought with a smile.

Adrian only moved a few hundred yards ahead this

time. He knew the similar time lapse between his two previous ambushes would have established a predictable rhythm to his attacks, at least in their minds. The faster interval time would catch them off guard.

They would also be watching their rear since the two attacks had come from that direction. Adrian would take them head on this time. He believed he could get the point man and the next one in line before they could react. Adrian could shoot, set another arrow, aim, and shoot again in just over three seconds. Because he was shooting instinctive style, no time was wasted in aiming with sights. He was also shooting for center of mass, a large target at these distances that was nearly impossible for him to miss. He heard the men coming and waited behind a tree directly in front of them on the path. He wanted them to see him this time. He wanted them to tell Wolfgang it was only one man bringing this war to him.

The point man walked into the optimum spot and the second was in easy range. Adrian stepped out from behind a tree with the bow already at full draw, shot instantly, reloaded, and shot again—both arrows true to target. Adrian then jumped swiftly across the trail and disappeared into the woods. He was in view for less than five seconds. The two men who had been shot grabbed at the arrows instead of shooting, a natural reaction. They blocked the man behind them from shooting. Adrian ran swiftly around and back, stepped out of the woods, and shot the final man of the eight. Adrian quickly disappeared back into the woods, out of sight and laughing uproariously, wanting them to hear him, which they did. They heard insane laughter from an obviously deranged man with long hair and a full beard, who appeared out of thin air dressed in buck-skins and bear fur, shot them with pointed sticks, then disappeared into the forest before they could react.

They gave up the mission. Adrian knew that even though the pointed arrows weren't immediately life threatening, they still hurt like hell. The wounds were mostly in muscle tissue, which would stiffen immediately after being hit. The more time that passed, the more it hurt. These men had no idea how much pain they were in for, but they knew they were hurting now and they knew they couldn't catch this damned ghost. So they reluctantly went back to camp. Telling Wolfgang how they had been humiliated wasn't going to be pleasant, but the fact that there were eight of them in the same position gave them some protection against his wrath, and appetite. Singling out one member now and then to make an example of was one thing. If he tried to punish eight of them at the same time he was liable to wake up alone the next morning. These men followed him because they chose to. They could just as easily choose not to and vote with their feet in the night.

Wolfgang was going to be extremely angry, even angrier because he could do nothing about it. This madman left him impotent with rage and embarrassment so intense that he would be unable to hide the humiliation from his men. This was just as Adrian intended.

CHAPTER 11

ADRIAN CIRCLED AROUND THE TRAIL the men had taken. He knew where they would exit the woods at the camp. He got into position to watch the camp as the men came into the opening. There were five of them. That meant the first three had already returned. Wolfgang would be furious when these five showed up without a prisoner. On cue, Wolfgang came out of his cabin stalking rigidly up to the men, meeting them as they came off the bridge.

Adrian watched the men stand with heads down as Wolfgang gestured wildly with his arms, his shouts carrying clear to his observation post. It was like watching theater to Adrian, and he was enjoying the show. He considered Wolfgang's options. He could abandon the camp, but that was not likely. Wherever they went, Adrian would simply follow them. They wouldn't be safer in town than they were in the woods. Wolfgang could send out more patrols; that seemed most likely. It was foolish and wouldn't accomplish anything other than to get more men wounded, but it was action and leaders were afraid of inaction, it made them look weak. Wolfgang really had no good options. Adrian was elusive in the woods and he had a sting, but at this point they weren't taking the sting seriously. They were just insulted.

The only point of reference they had for him was the cabin. He had abandoned it, and they might guess that he had, but they wouldn't know for sure. They certainly didn't know where else to look for him. Trying to find him in the woods would be a needle in a thousand haystacks operation. Worse, Adrian was a needle that actively bit back while moving its hiding place around. If they went out after him again it would be to the cabin again, but Adrian had a hunch they would take a different route. They would think it stupid to take the same route as before, and normally Adrian would agree, but in this case it made no difference. He would be there ambushing them whatever way they went.

Adrian chose the trail they would most likely take. He spent several hours that night making preparations, including making a crude grass dummy, then took up position near the trail the next morning. He chose a spot not far from the mining camp. If Wolfgang sent only a few men, Adrian might be able to send them back home quickly. If he sent a lot of men, it would take a little longer. Either way was fine; this was a war of attrition and nerves. Time was on Adrian's side, and he had no shortage of nerve.

Adrian watched as three men filed by him. They were moving along carelessly, noisily. They clearly didn't expect him to attack this close to the mining camp. It was amazing how foolish people could be. Just because the previous attacks had been further away, they assumed any more attacks would also be at the same distance. When the last man passed Adrian, he pulled on the cord next to him. The cord was strung through the woods and tied to the grass dummy. When the cord was pulled, the dummy was released to swing out and across the trail. The men saw what they thought was Adrian running across the trail in front of them. They began firing at the dummy immediately. While they were busy firing, Adrian stood and released three fast arrows. Then he disappeared into the woods. He hit all three; they were close and easy targets. By the time they turned to see where the arrows had come from, he was gone. Adrian ran toward the camp. He hoped that the close by gunfire would draw more men down the trail—and it did.

Four men came running down the trail at full tilt, weapons in front of them, cocked and ready. Again he waited until they passed by, stepped out, and released two arrows. They found homes in the meat of the men's backs. Adrian stepped back into the woods and ran forward, swiftly and silently, to get ahead of the four men. When he had passed by their position he returned to the trail. The four men were gathered in a knot, facing out in all directions, guns at the ready. No problem, Adrian only needed to stick the arrows into them; it didn't make much difference where. He lined the men up behind a short sapling and squatted down out of sight of the men, then fired two quick arrows over it. The arc of the arrows carried them up and then down into the cluster of men. By only partially drawing the bow he could adjust the arc and use the bow from out of sight. It wasn't the most accurate way to shoot, but it worked. The effect was also psychological: it was extremely demoralizing to the targets to have silent arrows fly in out of nowhere. His volley wounded one new man and put a second arrow into another.

Adrian shifted over thirty yards, lined up, and let fly two more arrows. He missed with both, but they were close. He could hear the men panicking, not knowing when or where the next arrows would come from. Adrian moved back towards the camp, staying alongside the trail. These men would return or more would come— either way was fine with him. The panicked men soon came running by, heading for camp as fast as possible. One was still unwounded. Adrian drew and let fly, hitting the man high in the back of his shoulder.

Adrian figured they wouldn't send more men out for a while, so he returned to his vantage point to watch the show. He reached the observation point after the men had all returned. The camp looked like a hornets' nest that had been kicked, men scurrying everywhere. They were taking positions where they could watch the forest, each with a rifle. They acted as if they were expecting Adrian to charge the camp with a knife between his teeth, waving a sword and Jolly Roger flag in his hand. Adrian laughed and enjoyed the show.

That night, Wolfgang put out a heavy guard. Men were roaming in and out between the buildings. Unfortunately, they were out of bow range of the woods. Adrian thought about sneaking in and sticking a few more of them; it would be easy in the dark. But instead he decided to leave them alone for a couple of days to build the tension. He walked the several miles to one of his food caches, pulling a bag of bear pemmican from a tree. Then he retrieved the hunting rifle and ammunition he had taken from his dead assailant.

He carried them back to his vantage point. Before daylight returned he built a low lean-to with dead wood and fresh tree branches. It provided shelter and camouflage. He lay inside the shelter, watching the sub-humans. It was a good time to learn more about them. The rifle was loaded with the safety off, ready to go. From this range he could pick the men off as fast as he could aim and pull the trigger. Not that he wanted to use it. But if things changed, he might have to leave the Stone Age and return to the rifle. If so, he would be ready.

Adrian watched for three days, without attacking, as the camp settled into a routine of sorts. The guards remained posted as heavily as before. No one went into the woods. He had no way of knowing how long their food supply would last, but given their poor woodcraft skills he doubted that they had been able to kill a lot of meat. He also doubted that they would have obtained a lot of food from the few local people. His best guess was that with as many mouths to feed as they had, it wouldn't be long before they were forced to venture out and find food.

He could also tell that over the past three days, the wounded had begun falling ill, slowly succumbing to the poison's doom. One of the cabins had been emptied of healthy men and turned into a hospital ward. It was a smart move to separate the wounded and dying from the healthy, but it didn't fool anyone. They had by now realized that the arrows were poisoned, and that what had seemed almost trivial wounds were in fact lethal. The diabolical nastiness of the poison arrow attacks was eating at the men's morale. They didn't understand this level of hatred, or why it was directed at them.

If it weren't for the eyewitness accounts, they would have sworn there were dozens of men waiting in the forest. The fact that it was one lone man had them badly shaken. A dozen men they could find and fight. One man, good at woodcraft, was near impossible to deal with. Over time he could pick them off one by one. He could get tired of playing with bows and arrows and start using one of the rifles they had not recovered. That might seem preferable to some of the men, since the crazy man so far was killing anyone he cared to kill slowly and painfully. At least a bullet would be a quick end.

After three days of increasing terror, they sent out four hunting parties with three men in each. Adrian knew that three men could take short night watch shifts. Three men could watch out for each other far better than two, and just as well as four or more. Three men wouldn't get in each other's way when hunting. Three men could travel quickly and quietly. Adrian respected the three-man team decision. He assumed that only half these teams were actually out to hunt elk to help feed the men back at camp. He suspected that two of the teams were out to look for him. He knew where the elk were, so he knew where these men would have to go to find them.

Though he doubted that these men knew where the elk were. They probably went into the woods and wandered around at random, looking for tracks in the snow. They might blunder on elk, or they might not get within miles of them. If Wolfgang's men were hungry and didn't get food soon, they would be forced to leave the mining camp, no doubt to raid the village. In fact it was inevitable that sooner or later they would hit the village up for food, since pillaging was in their nature.

Adrian decided to allow them to hunt. It would give them a couple more days to wonder if he was still at war with them or not. Adrian could spend the rest of his life carrying on this war. He was in no hurry, had no plans of going anywhere. In his mind they had snatched him from blessed relief, planning to torture him for information. He had never actively hated anyone before, but he hated these men with a cold, unrelenting rage. Adrian was intelligent, but he did not understand that this hatred was his mind's way of dealing with pain of Alice's death. Hatred is an anodyne.

The hunters did not return that night. It was a sign that they had not killed meat, or had killed it so late in the day they didn't have time to get back. The two groups that were most likely snooping around the abandoned cabin would be looking for a trail to pick up. They were out of luck. All of the tracks that could have led them to Adrian were gone thanks to the periodic snowfalls. Adrian was looking forward to spring. He would be able to hunt them more aggressively. He wouldn't leave tracks once the snow was gone, and it would be easier to hide when the foliage was more abundant.

As Adrian slept that night, a lone deserter snuck out of camp. He'd had enough. The screams from the dying men were penetrating his cabin wall all night, every night. When it was his turn to tend to the wounded, the stench of the gangrenous, putrefying flesh in the room was beyond nauseating. The room smelled like a pile of rotten meat after several days in the hot sun. It was ghastly. He was supposed to return to medic duty in the morning, but he couldn't take it again. He deserted instead. Even though he was taking a chance on becoming one of those screaming men if he ran into the insane archer, he had to get away.

Much later, Adrian would learn that this deserter had spread the word of Adrian's war on Wolfgang, creating a rapidly spreading legend and making a mythological hero of Adrian. It was hero worship that Adrian didn't want and damn well knew he didn't deserve. He slept that night as the seed of his legend slipped away into the dark forest, but he didn't sleep peacefully.

CHAPTER 12

TWO FULL DAYS PASSED BEFORE all four of the hunting parties were back. They had brought in two elk, a lot of meat. And, disgustingly, their haul also contained a human carcass. It wouldn't last that many men long, though. Fresh hunting parties were sent right back out. This time, Adrian expected they would all go for elk or humans, and with directions from the previous hunters, they should be back with meat relatively quickly. He didn't think they would keep looking for him; he hadn't done anything to them in several days, and had left no tracks. By now they were thinking he had left, or something had happened to him putting him out of action. Psychological warfare on this level was pretty simple. Demoralize the men, keep them pinned down by their own fear, then pick them off one at a time until they were all gone. Or until they turned inwards on themselves and finished the job for him.

It was about mental leverage. He had the leverage. He could move freely and easily and strike from a thousand places. They were big, easy targets. They knew that every time they went into the woods they risked not just death, but slow, painful death. Giving them several days of peace and quiet had lessened the tension; now it was time to let them know he was still here. Let them know he was toying with them as he pleased. This would ratchet up their fear far beyond where it had been before.

These men were, like men everywhere, creatures of habit. They had three well-defined footpaths they used to travel in and out of camp. As the trails went further into the woods, they branched and branched again until each individual trail disappeared—like tree limbs, then branches, then twigs. It was functional and efficient, but it made for poor security. Good security meant entering the woods at different places each time, avoiding the habitual use of a singular trail to the point that it became worn and obvious. Even now, while under threat, they still used these trails. Adrian thought it would be interesting to try to train them to avoid all but one trail, just to see if they could be manipulated so easily.

With the simple objective of inflicting contaminated puncture wounds, there were two easily made traps that would be effective on these trails: punji pits and swipes. Punji pits were small holes dug in the ground. The diameter only needed to be enough to fit a grown man's foot—eighteen inches in diameter was a good size. They only had to be about fourteen inches deep. After digging the pit, the excess soil is carefully placed on a piece of leather and carried off so as to not leave any fresh dirt to attract attention. Sharpened sticks were driven into the bottom of the pit, sharp end up. Cover the sharpened punji stakes with dung, then cover the hole with something flimsy, like small twigs. Lay bark over the twigs and cover them with the same dirt and leaves that covers the rest of the trail. When done properly it was near impossible to see. After a snowfall, they were simply undetectable.

Sooner or later, one of Wolfgang's men would come along, walking as he normally would, without scrutinizing the ground below. As his foot passed through the flimsy covering and he shifted his weight onto it, the sharpened stakes, placed at various angles, would impale his foot and leg. The stakes had the same barbs cut into them, making it impossible to remove them and leave a clean wound channel. The infection followed just as with the arrows.

Adrian placed a few punji pits at random, but the first few were strategically located to improve the odds that the men would pass over them. One of Adrian's favorite spots was behind a log that had to be stepped over. Between roots or rocks that the men had to navigate around also worked well. Sometimes there would be a sharp bend in the trail—another good place. Once the targets knew to watch, though, they watched those places, making them no longer effective. The randomly placed ones kept the targets on edge and sometimes worked. The downside of the punji pits was that the wounds were typically inflicted on an extremity which could be amputated, saving the man's life. On the other hand, the sight of a man with only one foot hanging around camp was sufficiently demoralizing in and of itself. Not to mention, the amputee would be out of action, and another useless mouth to feed.

Swipes were tree branches or saplings that could be pulled back and tied off, then connected to a trip line. When released, they sprang back to their original position, smacking the person that tripped the cord. They didn't hit with enough force to cause serious damage, but the sharpened stakes tied to them hit hard enough for their sharp points to penetrate. These were made the same way as the punji stakes. Swipes were relatively easy to spot because the trip lines were difficult to hide. They were best placed in sharp curves, or creek crossings. They were also easily disengaged by wind and animals. Still they were effective, especially psychologically.

Adrian spent all night rigging two of the trails with both types of trap. After he had tricked up the first half-mile of each, he set traps parallel to the trails. He knew that the men would, after half a mile, decide that walking the trail was no longer a viable option, but being lazy they would try to walk next to it. He chose places where moving off the trail to the side was inviting—game trails or natural breaks in the brush. The men would soon learn that being anywhere near these trails would be dangerous. Swipes were much harder to detect off the trail, but quick and easy to create.

The other terrifying thing about these traps is they could be put anywhere. The men that he was hunting knew this. It would make them move slowly and extremely carefully after a few men had been wounded. But Adrian could move freely; the traps would work when he was miles away. It could make the simple act of leaving or returning to camp a game of Russian roulette. Twelve men would be returning to camp soon, using one of the three trails or the road. Two of the trails had been heavily booby-trapped. Adrian left one trail and the gravel road clear, for now.

Adrian waited in the woods for two days before one of the groups returned. He waited near one of the two trapped trails, out past the last of the traps. The six men who took this path had been successful, each carrying a large load of meat by backpack. They were walking slowly; Adrian could see they were tired. After the last in line passed, Adrian he shot him in the buttocks since the meat was protecting his back. He only shot one arrow, then faded into the woods. He moved forward and came back to the trail ahead of the men. In only a few minutes they came by him again, moving fast, leaving the wounded man to hobble along and fend for himself. "Nice," Thought Adrian. "Real nice. No loyalty for each other. They're treating him like a dead man already."

Adrian shot an arrow into the last man in line. Then he hiked cross country to the other trail he had rigged with traps. The men he had just left would be expecting him to hound them all the way to camp. They would be panicked and going as fast as they could. Their quick and careless travel would mean more of them would be snagged by booby-traps along the way. Pretty soon they would be in sheer terror, looking desperately for traps and waiting for arrows to fly silently out of the forest. His tactics were intended to create terror as well as kill.

Adrian traveled cross-country to perform the same tactics against the other men if they came down the one of the other booby-trapped trails. He waited until dark, but no one showed. Either they hadn't come back yet, or they had taken a different route. He had one more little trick to play before daylight, and then he would rest the following day. He walked back to the mining camp, avoiding trails as he always did. He was careful to leave as few tracks as he could in the snow. The snow on the ground was his worst enemy. If the cannibals ever got a lead on him it would be because of the tracks he left. He timed most of his movements for just before and during snow storms, so that fresh snow would cover his tracks.

This wasn't always practical, though.

When he had no fresh snow to depend on, he used rocks and streams as much as possible. There were windswept places where snow was blown off the rocks, places he could use to his advantage. Better yet were the many streams in the mountains. He could walk up and down them on the ice and not leave any mark. If the weather warmed enough that the ice melted, then he walked in the water. This was cold work, but effective. It meant that he had to build a fire that night to dry his feet and boots, though, so he had to camp out far away from the mining camp. His best bet by far was to hole up during the pretty, still days and travel during the snow flurries. This required careful navigation and knowing all the local landmarks intimately.

He traveled up and downhill using streams and cross terrain to cover his tracks, or rocks where he could. Effectively this meant that he left tracks on the side-slope portions of his area of travel, tracks that went from stream to stream. A tracker could follow him to a stream and then go up or down it. They might find a few tracks high up among the rocks, but then the tracks would disappear at another stream. A skilled and dedicated tracker could follow him, eventually. That tracker would have to move slowly to get all the clues, and would be under constant threat of ambush. Adrian didn't think they had any skilled trackers as he had seen no signs yet that anyone had come close to finding him. He also thought that even if they had someone clever enough to work out the tracks they didn't have anyone brave enough to face the threat of constant ambush.

Adrian watched the camp from the woods until the stars told him it was around four in the morning. Then he snuck into the mining camp for the first time. Getting past the sentries was easy; they were mostly asleep. The difficult part was making no noise while digging. Using the trowel he had found by the upper mine, he slowly and silently dug a punji pit in front of the door to the hospital cabin. He placed contaminated punji stakes in the hole, then covered it. When he was done it looked just like the bare earth that it had been before, a worn spot in front of a cabin door does not attract close inspection. Or it hadn't before now. After tomorrow they would never walk in or out of the cabins again with looking hard at the ground.

He had chosen the hospital cabin because defiling it would be exceptionally insulting. The fact that he could sneak in, dig a hole, set a trap and get back out past the sentries was bad enough. That he would sneak in and out, and set a punji pit right in their camp, was extremely bad. But to do it where wounded men were being cared for spoke of a mind that was unhinged, beyond moral redemption, insane or pure evil—maybe both. This one brazen act would create a terror in their minds that would haunt them at night as they tried, and failed, to sleep. Adrian knew in a calculated way exactly what he was accomplishing. Up until now they had felt relatively safe in camp. Even that small measure of comfort would be gone in the morning.

He returned to his lean-to vantage point before dawn and waited. Smoke appeared out of the chimneys at day break as fires were built to warm the cabins, but no one came outside for another half hour. Then the men started coming out and heading for the outhouses. Breakfast was cooking. Adrian could smell roasting meat from where he was. It disgusted him that some of it was human flesh, but he realized that he hadn't eaten all day. He pulled the par fleche to him and dug in. The bear pemmican was delicious.

As he chewed he watched a man carrying a bucket of water to the hospital cabin reach for the door and step right into the punji pit. His scream jarred the camp into action as men ran to the cabins to grab rifles. The sentries stood and moved to take cover, aiming their rifles out at the line of trees around the camp. Pandemonium broke loose for several minutes before anyone discovered that the man had been injured by a trap. Adrian could read fury on the men's faces, even at that distance. Their sharp movements spoke eloquently of their rage.

Wolfgang armed twenty men with long sticks, and then had them sweep the camp from end to end and side to side, poking at the ground looking for more traps. None were found. This became a morning ritual every day. The long sticks were stacked against the outsides of the cabins and every morning the men would take them up and check the entire camp for traps before anyone else came out. Adrian loved it. With one small trap he had permanently changed their behavior, complicating their lives with even more fear.

Wolfgang had a bad evening followed by a bad morning. The previous evening he had four men come in with poisoned wounds. Two from Adrian's arrows and two from booby traps. Even the trails themselves could no longer be trusted. Then came the injury by a trap in his own camp. He was furious and would have happily killed Adrian a thousand times, yet for the life of him he couldn't figure out how to find him.

CHAPTER 13

ADRIAN WATCHED THE CAMP FOR the rest of the day. After dark he left his vantage point and returned to the trails. He rebuilt the punji pits that had been stepped in. It only took a few minutes to freshen them up, and these men might be stupid enough to step in the same trap twice, so why not? He then moved over to the third trail and put traps alongside it. Eventually he was hoping to force the men to use this trail, or the road, whenever they left camp. It would take a while, but they would eventually notice that there were no traps on this trail or the road. They might notice that there were traps off each side of them. They would wonder why he was leaving them safe lanes of travel, and probably conclude that it was for his own use. They would be extra slow and careful but they would still use them, or else walk into the woods where there were no trails. Given what he had seen so far of them, he didn't think they would take to the woods without a trail. To help make sure they didn't venture into the woods, he placed traps in in the most likely paths they would use if they decided to avoid the trails.

Adrian had no way of trapping the road. It was an all-weather road made of gravel compacted into an iron-like surface from years of truck traffic. There were potholes, but men on foot would avoid them naturally, so punji pits weren't an option. They would simply walk down the center of the road avoiding any kind of swipe traps. He placed traps parallel to the road, lots of them. If they wandered off the road, he wanted them to return right back to it. He had a reason for that. If he could increase the traffic on the road by decreasing it on the other trails, he would be more effective at hit and run ambushes along the road. More traffic meant more opportunities.

While Adrian was attacking out in the woods, it probably had not occurred to Wolfgang that he was also spending time to watching the camp. Now that he had attacked the camp itself, if Wolfgang had any sense, he would know that Adrian was watching the camp from the wood line. Once he came to that conclusion, the only rational reaction would be to search the wood line for tracks, and to establish a roving patrol that circled the camp just inside the wood line in hopes of finding him. It was only a matter of time before his lean-to vantage point was discovered.

With that in mind, Adrian began setting traps around his vantage point. He used every natural opening in the brush, every game trail, every feature a man was likely to follow or investigate. He placed so many traps that it was difficult for him to get in and out, and he knew where they all were. They might find this spot, but they would pay a price in the process. Because of the bowl shape of the camp, Adrian had virtually endless choices around the camp from which to watch. He set up dummy camps in the less desirable spots, and then heavily booby-trapped them.

He had the men so scared of the forest that he could move around during the day with near impunity. He placed traps in the woods completely around the camp. The roving patrols would be bound within a certain distance of the camp; in that band of area there were natural places where a man could walk, and places where the terrain or thickets made walking impossible. The terrain and the vegetation created bottlenecks, narrow places that were the only passages from one area to another. Adrian took advantage of all of these places. Within a week he had placed so many traps that he was having difficulty remembering where they were. He found it easier to avoid the areas completely, and leaving himself safe lanes to travel away from the booby traps.

It took Wolfgang four days to figure out what Adrian had been waiting for. He sent out two roving patrols of two men each. They were apparently ordered to move around the perimeter of the camp, inside the wood line, in opposite directions, crossing each other's path twice each full circle. It was a clever method of patrolling. Two men were sufficient in each patrol. These men were literally only meant to give warning to the camp by shooting at Adrian. Wolfgang would not expect them to actually get Adrian, although he could hope. Upon hearing shots fired another group would immediately follow the sounds of gunfire to the source and then chase and kill Adrian. The plan was easy for Adrian to figure out; a group of ten armed men were always in the picnic building ready to go. They were obviously a strike team waiting for a signal. This gave Adrian an idea.

The first day of the perimeter patrol was a disaster for Wolfgang. All four of the men were stabbed with poison stakes in one way or another. The traps were deadly effective in the brush. Adrian's plan to set the traps where the men would be forced to walk worked perfectly. Adrian watched from one of his many vantage points. He could not cover his tracks around the perimeter, so instead he made so many tracks that they couldn't be untangled. The patrols' tracks would soon cover so much territory that even an expert tracker would be confused.

The next day four new men moved out into perimeter patrol. Moving slowly, they carried big sticks which they flailed at the ground and brush in front of them as they went. Eventually they cleared a path that they could walk, but they were also forced to stay on it, making them easy to avoid. For all intents and purposes the patrol was useless once they stayed strictly on the same path all the time. Each night Adrian would place a few new traps on their path to force them to repeat the stick exercise each morning. It only took one near miss for them to realize that he was operating on their trail after they had retreated to their cabins. They continued the patrol—it would be an admission of failure to stop—but they knew it was an exercise in futility. That knowledge increased the effectiveness of Adrian's operation. He had them acting like trained monkeys, and they knew it, but they couldn't stop themselves. He was reminded of how in the grid days, terrorists had radically and permanently changed Americans' behavior at airports, with just one attack. It was amazing how their fear of him, and their reluctance to go into the woods without a trail, was working to shape their behavior patterns.

Adrian had the men trapped in the camp, except for the hunting parties. If they left and returned by the untouched trail or road, he left them alone. He wanted them to have food; he did not want them to have to raid the village. He didn't want them hunting humans, but they had been doing it before he arrived, and surely the people in their area knew it and took defensive actions. Wolfgang would want to raid the village, and would sooner or later, but Adrian wasn't going to force the issue. When they did go on a raid, they would use the road, and he would harass and ambush them mercilessly. He believed that he could mortally wound as many as twenty to thirty men if they took to the road in a large number.

It had been nearly two weeks since Adrian had first penetrated the camp's security. It was time to do it again, and ratchet up their fear another notch. They still put sentries out each night, armed men that took up positions around the camp. Adrian observed that they habitually used the same positions every night, and changed guards at the same time every night. This was another example of poor security. They were acting in predictable patterns that anyone could take advantage of. And Adrian certainly would. He waited for dark.

He had made a war club, a smooth river rock shaped like a small loaf of bread. Using a harder stone he rubbed an indentation around the center of the rock all the way around it. Splitting a piece of green hardwood he placed the groove into the split, then laced it together with wraps of rawhide. He dried the rawhide and the green handle next to his fire each time he built one. Within a few days the club was phenomenally strong and extremely deadly. The head was like a two-pound hammer. The handle was two-and-a-half feet long and big enough around that it fit Adrian's hand perfectly. He had cut the handle to a length that balanced the club's swing. It would crush a skull with a flick of his wrist. It would bust a head into shattered pieces with a half-swing. A full swing would leave mush where a head had once been. And it was totally silent.

At four in the morning, Adrian's favorite time for attack, he moved stealthily into the camp. He had chosen a route that none of the sentries could see. He could have walked in carrying a lantern and they wouldn't have had any idea if they stayed where they were. It was pure stupidity on their part, but each man wanted to have as many walls around him as possible. They were scared to be out in the open, where they should have been after dark.

He rose up behind the first of the guards like the grim reaper he had become, and with a half-swing crushed the man's head in so thoroughly that the man's body fell straight down without twitching. The sound of his crumpling body was too quiet to alert the other guards. Adrian knew exactly where each one was. He moved quietly and calmly to the next guard. This one was asleep, breathing in that deep, relaxed way that only the truly asleep do. Adrian decided to leave him alive, for now. Instead of killing him, he placed one of his arrows across his lap, so that he would know how close he had come to dying in his sleep. His tale would bring more terror than his body; there would be enough bodies.

Adrian left the sleeping man to dream his dreams. He put his hand against the cabin wall to orient himself as he walked to the next guard. This one was awake, but yawning. Adrian moved forward swiftly, drawing his club up over his shoulder while the man was in mid-yawn, a particularly vulnerable moment. Before he had a chance to finish the yawn, the stone came down through the top of his head, smashing through the skull and the brain, stopping only when it reached the shoulders.

Adrian grabbed the dead man's body to help ease it to the ground; no need for noise.

Adrian move from guard to guard, abruptly ending their lives with a flick of his wrist, a flashing blur of stone, until he had killed all but the one. Five bodies would be found in the morning. One live guard with an arrow to show and a story to tell to all the others. Adrian thought, "This is Stone Age war at its finest." The gruesomeness of the smashed heads would be a gory testament to how strong their adversary was.

Adrian boldly walked away from the camp. There was no one to see him. It would be the last night that any of Wolfgang's men would go outside after dark. From now on they would lock themselves in their cabins as soon as the sun went down, in fear of the monster that preyed upon them in the dark, and in the woods, and roamed through their camp at will. As bad a shape as he was leaving them in, he had another idea for tomorrow that would make things even worse.

CHAPTER 14

HEN THE MEN CAME OUT to get their sticks to sweep the camp for punji pits the next morning they found the five dead guards, and the one live one. The arrow was handed from hand to hand as each man looked at the bodies lying in a row, their heads smashed into gory shreds. There was a somberness among them. Where they had gestured wildly the morning of the punji pit, they looked defeated today. There was no anger evident, no sharp gestures, no frantic running around. Just men with slumped shoulders standing in small groups, talking. Adrian's strike had taken a lot out of them, the cumulative compounding of terror on top of terror was reaching an apex. Pretty soon these men would fall into a deep dark depression relieved only by moments of terror.

The two roving patrols were sent out as usual, plus two more. They took up sticks and began searching their tried and true lanes for fresh traps. They would find two. Adrian hadn't had time last night to put out more. Two was enough to keep them anxious. Four patrols were too many for Adrian's newest idea. He would wait and see if they dropped back to two. He thought they might at lunchtime. The extra patrols were a gesture by Wolfgang, a useless gesture that wasn't worth pursuing. Adrian settled in to watch, and to avoid the roving patrols, which was easy since they stayed on their cleared path religiously.

At lunchtime all four patrols came in to eat with the rest of the men. Then, only two patrols were sent back out. The rest of the men were busy fortifying the cabins. They were building shutters for the windows and wooden bars that could be dropped into place inside the doors to lock them. Now that he had demonstrated a free run of the camp they were worried that he would begin coming into the cabins as well. Adrian had no intention of doing that. In order to keep these men at maximum terror, they needed to believe they had one small, safe place they could go. If he took that safe place away from them then there would be little else to take from them and they would be more likely to abandon the camp. He wanted them to have their safe place, and to fear its loss with every breath they took. It was more effective to leave them some small hope, false as it may be, than to take away all shreds of it.

Adrian knew he could set fire to the cabins any night he wanted. But he liked this camp. It made his war easy. If he burned the cabins, they would have to move, and the next place might not be as good. When he saw that only two patrols were back on duty, he decided to execute his next plan. The strike team was poised and ready to go. Twelve armed men would rush to the sounds of gunfire, hoping to find and shoot Adrian. Each man would be dreaming of being the one who killed Adrian, ending the war. That man would be a hero.

They had not practiced their tactics at all. Adrian knew they would be stumbling all over each other when they ran toward the gunfire. They would not have discipline. They would all be running on hair-trigger adrenalin surges. They would be afraid of getting a poison arrow or stake in them and dying the slow death in the grim cabin. They would shoot at anything that moved. That was what Adrian was counting on.

He had prepared his lean-to vantage point with dozens of booby traps in hopes that the patrols would discover it, move in, and set off the traps, injuring more of them. They hadn't found it. It was time to show it to them. Taking a pistol that he had picked up after one of the wounded men left it in the forest; he walked into a position that placed the lean-to camp between him and the strike force. Then he waited for the roving patrol to be as close to that spot as they were going get. When they were, he fired the pistol in their direction, shooting all the bullets in the clip. He yelled at the same time, "There he is! I see him! Red shirt! Red shirt!" One of the men on patrol was wearing a red shirt.

The twelve men sprinted directly towards the gunfire, stringing out as the faster men gained on the slower ones. The patrol whirled and headed towards the gunfire also, reaching the spot just moments before the first members of the strike team arrived. Adrian had faded back into the woods and chosen a place where he could watch without being seen. As the men all started to converge on the same place, two of the men in the strike team began shooting at the man in the red shirt. The man in the red shirt began shooting back. Within seconds there was chaos as men shot at each other and returned fire. Several were wounded in the fracas, but none killed outright. Then men began stumbling into Adrian's traps. Fourteen men filled with adrenalin and a small area filled with traps is a bad combination. Adrian couldn't tell how many were punctured, but from the yells and reactions it appeared that several had been.

The man in the red shirt had been shot twice; it didn't look like he would live to get back to camp. At least three other men had been badly wounded by the errant rifle fire from the confused and excited men. It was a disaster for Wolfgang. His men, thoroughly demoralized, terrorized, and panicky, had been easily duped into attacking each other when their mission had been to kill Adrian. They began to return to camp, heads bowed, shoulders slumped, defeated in every way possible. Adrian slipped up closer and let fly three arrows, hitting two of the men and barely missing a third. He turned and disappeared back into the woods, laughing.

Some of the men, enraged beyond sanity by their situation, heard his laughter, turned, and charged back into the forest after him. They stumbled onto yet more booby-traps, another one of them getting a poison puncture wound before they gave up again and went back to camp.

Wolfgang gathered the uninjured men who had just returned and picked out several more from the camp. They armed up and followed Wolfgang into the woods again, entering at the same spot as before. Using long sticks they slowly and methodically began clearing the area in front of them as they walked deeper into the woods where Adrian had disappeared. Wolfgang was intent on finding Adrian; it didn't matter how long it took or how many men he lost in the process. If he didn't find Adrian and kill him, he was going to lose all the men, and soon.

The only reason they didn't desert him now was because they were afraid to go into the woods. They were stuck in the camp.

The snow was covered with tracks. The beltway that the roving guards used was useless for tracking. There were so many tracks inside it that the snow was nearly worn away. Wolfgang went deeper into the forest, heading in the opposite direction of the tracks. Adrian watched from a distance. He noticed that Wolfgang was taking a slow and steady approach to this business. He was leading his men in a wide line as they looked for tracks. Whenever one of the men spotted something everyone stopped where they were while Wolfgang went to investigate. If it was nothing important they continued the way they were going, but if it was interesting then the whole line shifted to center on the new track and followed in whatever direction Wolfgang thought it was going. It was a good procedure, and one that would eventually work if it didn't snow again. It also gave Adrian ample opportunity to ambush and shoot more men. However, there was a problem now: Wolfgang wouldn't run away like his men had in the past. It was Adrian's fault, of course. He had pushed Wolfgang to the point that running away was no more appealing than moving forward—but moving forward had a shred of hope attached to it. Wolfgang would be willing to lose all of these men, and to summon more and lose them too. Now, if Adrian shot at the men, they would turn and follow the arrow's path, find his fresh tracks, and soon they'd be on close on his trail.

It didn't look like it was going to snow anytime soon. He was now the hunted, perhaps because he had pushed too hard. It didn't matter why at this point. The problem was a tactical one. Attack or retreat? Both options had pros and cons. Attacking would take out more men; perhaps they would break and run, perhaps not, but more men out meant more men out. Retreating, on the other hand, meant he was far less likely to be found, and would be able to come back when the conditions were in his favor. He could return and do more damage, demoralize them further. Realistically, it was time to retreat and wait. He had created a great deal of havoc and damage in the past few days. He could afford to wait for better weather conditions before striking again.

Adrian began moving away from the men toward a frozen creek not too far away. He would walk up the ice, leaving no tracks. When he reached the timberline he would find the band of windswept rocks that would help him to move without tracks across country, then he would go down another frozen stream, cross to yet another stream, and move back up. Once he did this enough times he would lose the men following him. Then he could hole up in a temporary shelter, build a fire, eat bear pemmican, and rest. He could use the sleep. When a storm came in he would move back down and pick off a few more men, set a few more traps. It was a good plan.

Adrian reached the stream. The ice was half frozen and slushy. He couldn't walk on it; he would sink into it and leave tracks in it. The ice would freeze again after dark, making the tracks last for days. He kept on moving. He needed to go on to the next stream over. It was smaller, and would be better ice. He did the best he could to hide his tracks in between. Brushing them out with a pine bough did not work, it just made a mess of the snow that anyone could see. He quickly realized that speed was going to serve him better than trying to hide his tracks down here. He might hide a few, but there would be too many remaining that would be found. Adrian picked up the pace.

The next stream was in better shape. The ice was solid enough to walk on without leaving tracks. He knew that Wolfgang would find this point sometime today, maybe late in the evening. They would probably camp here and follow on in the morning. They couldn't follow him in the dark. Adrian could move well in the dark. He followed the ice all the way up to the timber line, and then some. When he found an outcropping of rock he followed it to the South a hundred yards, leaving only small edges of tracks here and there. Then he turned and came back to the ice without leaving a trace, and followed it another half-mile. This time he left the ice on a small shelf of rocks. It would be extremely difficult to walk on the shelf without leaving tracks. The East bound trail had been a diversion. He was Westbound and he didn't think they would believe that he could take this route and leave no trace. Adrian believed that they would lose his trail, or find the false trail and follow it, but they would never find the true trail. Adrian hadn't been wrong in a long time; he was overdue for an error.

CHAPTER 15

BOVE THE TIMBERLINE THE SKY was an open, vast field of intense blue. A few clouds highlighted the sky's color with their contrasting white. It was a bluebird day. Out in the sun it was warm, as long as he kept moving. He had to stop and remove clothing to keep from sweating. Carrying the clothing was a bother as it occupied one arm that could be better used to keep his balance. Adrian finally stopped, and using leather cords, made the buffalo robe into a bundle he slung over his back like a bedroll. It changed his center of balance to have that weight on his back, and that took getting used to. Still, it was better to have both hands free. Keeping his footing on slippery rocks was difficult business. Falling would be seriously bad up here. Once he started rolling downhill he might not stop for a long time, and bouncing off of rocks was a surefire way to get badly injured.

It felt good to be out of the dark forest and in the bright sunlight. How beautiful the view was up here. Long vistas of snow covered mountains and valleys greeted his eyes whichever direction he looked. He hadn't realized that he had been getting claustrophobic down in the forest, where all he could see was trees and brush and occasional meadows. It was dark in the forest. Even when the sun was at its highest it barely penetrated down to the forest floor. Daylight was short too; the mountains cut the morning and evenings off abruptly. Getting out from the dense trees for a while was a much-needed break. He was enjoying the view, and moving along nicely.

He thought that he had a solid day-and-a-half head start on Wolfgang. This time of year that should be more than enough. It rarely went more than three days without snowing some, but it hadn't snowed in many days now. Snow was due. Once snow returned, he would return with it, and wreak havoc on the camp. He was the dog of war, and he had been let slip. Adrian smiled at this twist on one of his favorite quotes. Adrian hadn't smiled at anything except his enemy's misery in a long time. A true smile of pleasure felt strange, made him feel peculiar. He stopped smiling abruptly. A man at war had no time for such things. He returned to thinking about his next steps.

His very next step was to get to the nearest frozen stream without leaving any tracks leading to it. He concentrated on placing his foot on the next spot that would provide solid footing and not leave a track. Then he concentrated on the next one, and so on. It was a good way to move, as quickly as caution would allow. His senses were tuned to his surroundings. He heard a distant eagle's cry, smelled the sun-warmed rocks. He stopped occasionally and looked all around him, searching for anything that didn't belong. Then he went back to picking his stepping spots.

Adrian reached the frozen stream after noon. He had been steadily traveling since the day before. He had traveled by moonlight most of the night, stopping only when the moon went too low to give adequate light. He had slept about an hour, huddled in his bearskin robe. No fire could be built up here, it would be seen for miles. When he got to the stream, he sat down to eat. The sun at this altitude could turn skin into burnt meat. To help prevent sunburn, he rubbed the fatty bear pemmican on his face, hands, arms, and neck—any part of him that might be exposed to the high concentration of ultraviolet light in the thin atmosphere. He ate more of the pemmican, not out of hunger, but for fuel. He enjoyed the meat tremendously, but the high altitude made his appetite disappear. He ate for fuel, knowing his body needed it.

Adrian began moving down the frozen stream. This was more difficult than going uphill on the ice. When going uphill, he leaned forward into the slope, which gave him a better center of gravity. If he fell it would only be a short distance and his feet would be toe down, making it easier to stop a slide. Going downhill was the opposite. He leaned backwards slightly to prevent his center of gravity from getting too far ahead of him, causing a loss of balance. If he fell, he fell further, and his feet would be toe up. There was the danger of a runaway slide down the ice, which he wouldn't be able to stop before he had gained so much momentum that stopping became a danger in itself. It was an effort that required total concentration. Total concentration was dangerous when a man was being hunted. It meant that he wasn't able to watch out for his enemies, who Adrian believed were far behind. They weren't. Not all of them.

He had forgotten about the men who were out hunting elk. They should have been far to the East where the elk herds were, but these men were not good hunters. Some of them thought hunting was a matter of randomly walking around hoping to spot something to shoot. Amateurs were the most dangerous people in the world. They did not do what they were supposed to do. They didn't know what they should be doing and therefore could be doing almost anything. They were unpredictable.

Adrian felt a stunning impact on the side of his head but no pain, vaguely heard the distant gunshot, as he fell and began sliding down the ice. "Shit," he thought. "That rifle shot will bring Wolfgang on the run, right to me. I lost all that time." Adrian was trying to check his slide. He needed to control his stop, not end up crushed against a boulder. The creek turned slightly to the right, but Adrian managed to keep going straight, over the creek bank and into a deep snow drift. He came to a stop buried in the snow.

He had bored a hole into the snow as he was driven into it, but it collapsed behind him. He was suffocating and could barely move his arms. Fortunately he had covered his head like a boxer with his arms in reaction to the sound of the bullet. He was now able to move his forearms back and forth, clearing a breathing space in front of his face. He had to keep moving; he had no idea how far away the shooter had been, but he was sure the man was rushing towards him as fast as he could. Adrian had to get out of this snow, or he would smother or freeze or get shot dead, whichever came first—and whichever came first was coming fast.

It was difficult to move his arms, but the snow wasn't tightly packed or more than a few feet deep. He kept moving his arms until he had cleared out a larger space around his head. He was disoriented. He couldn't tell which way was up. He felt dizzy from the blow to the head. He did not know which way to dig to get out. If he started digging in front of him, he might only dig deeper down into the bank. "Calm down. Think." He took three deep breaths then recalled hearing a story of a man in a similar situation. He did what that man had done. He made a small snowball and dropped it to see which way it fell—right into his face. He began digging upward and soon felt his hand break the surface. For all he knew his assailant was standing there watching his hand. If not, he soon would be.

Adrian dug as rapidly as he could and pulled himself out of the snow. It was a huge effort. His head pounded and ached and he was dizzy and becoming nauseous, but he drove himself to superhuman effort. It was extreme effort or death, and Adrian wasn't thinking about giving up, not now. His grief had slipped behind him somewhere in his insane war and all could think about was getting out so he could kill the man who had shot him, before that man shot him again.

Adrian stood up and was half free of the snow drift. He reached down and brought out his robe that had fallen off his back while he was trapped in the snow. He didn't have a gun. He was unarmed, facing a man with a rifle, in open country. He looked around and didn't see anyone. He closed his eyes and recreated the slam against his head and the shot he heard. About one second apart. The man was close, would be closer by now, much closer. Adrian stomped the snow down hard under him and threw the robe down beside the snowdrift, squatted down, and pulled loose snow back in on top of him. He held his stone club tightly in his right hand. The robe would draw the shooter up close. He would see it, along with the disturbed snow, and come to investigate. He would be cautious but curious.

When he got close enough Adrian would jump out of the snow from the squat position and try to take him. It could work. It had to work—it was all he had and the only plan that would come to his dizzy head. He waited for what seemed years, his legs cramping, his lungs heaving, his head spinning and nausea trying to sweet talk him into vomiting. He waited and waited. Finally he heard slow footsteps crunching in the snow. He bit the inside his cheek to distract from his painfully bent legs. The steps came closer. He heard the man clear his throat. He was close. He heard the man take a step closer.

Adrian shot up out of the snow bank and launched himself like a rocket in the direction of the sounds. He was already swinging the club in midair at the point he guessed the man's head to be. He was close. He blasted the man's left shoulder, crushing bones into gravel. The man screamed once as he dropped the rifle to grab his destroyed shoulder, and Adrian smashed him a backhanded return blow into the forehead and out the back of his skull. Brains, blood, bones, and hair rained into the snow behind the man as his body fell straight down. He was dead instantly.

Adrian fell onto his back into the snow as the trajectory of his launch carried him past the man's body. Adrian jumped up, grabbed the rifle, and hit the snow rolling. The hunters were often in pairs. He had to find the other man before he took a shot at Adrian. He rolled over and over to avoid being an easy target, then came to his feet looking around wildly. No one in sight. Adrian called out in a deliberately hoarse voice, "Got him, over here!" He waited—no response. He climbed a boulder and lay on top of, looking around. He saw the man's tracks coming in, and only his alone. Adrian was in luck, only the one hunter. He knew the shot had been heard by Wolfgang and that they would be coming here as fast as they could. Adrian figured that he had two hours, maybe three.

he had to get moving. First he sat down and carefully explored the side of his head with his cold fingers. It felt like the bullet had not penetrated into bone, but had scraped along the bone hard on the side of the head and gone on past, tearing up skin, leaving behind a concussion. Adrian's eyesight was blurry, more so in his right eye. His ears were ringing and he had the worst headache he could ever remember having. His military medical training told him he had a severe concussion and it would become worse as the brain swelled. He would be out of action for a week, maybe more; and that depended on him getting to some place safe where he could wait while his body healed. He had to move, find a good hiding spot. He had to find it fast because the swelling of the brain would soon cause him to lose consciousness. Had to push himself hard, but not leave tracks. He had to do it all quickly. He told himself all this, but it was several long minutes before his body responded.

It was like sending signals down a faulty wire. His muscles were receiving static; they didn't know what to do with the garbled information his brain was sending out. Somewhere beneath his conscious level the primitive part of his brain took over, sending clear signals. He stood up slowly and shakily, put his robe on, then took the rifle and ammo and the man's canteen. He began to slowly and cautiously move down the frozen creek, downhill, looking for a place to hide. This was the most danger he had been in since attacking the grizzly bear.

CHAPTER 16

ADRIAN STUMBLED FOREVER IN A white haze of pain and nausea. He fell on the ice so many times that he wasn't sure if he was crawling and occasionally stood up, or was walking but fell often. He just kept moving down the ice, into the woods, down the ice, down the ice. His only coherent thoughts were "down the ice" "hiding place" "move, move, move, move...". He was running on raw instinct as his brain swelled.

He had been clawing his way down the frozen stream for two hours, occasionally stopping to look for a place to hide. He knew that Wolfgang would be close behind somewhere. Even though he wasn't leaving tracks, there was no place else they needed to look. His tracks led to the ice and until he stepped off the ice, they wouldn't need to look elsewhere and they could travel fast. Adrian was freezing cold, his hands completely numb, his feet long forgotten. Light snow was falling—not good. He needed to find shelter, now.

Ahead he saw an overhanging creek bank in a bend. The overhanging earth was held together with tree roots. It formed a bit of overhead shelter as it hung out over the ice. Adrian crawled under it and looked up. He saw a large hole under the root ball into the bank. Roots were hanging down in front of the hole, making it near invisible. Only by crawling right up to it had Adrian seen it. He crawled closer. The hole seemed to go back like a cave. It was a large hole, big enough for Adrian to crawl into on his hands and knees, with a little room to spare. In his last moments of consciousness, he was careful not to disturb anything; he didn't leave any dirt on the ice. He crawled into the hole and disappeared from the world. It was warmer in the hole. Not warm by any stretch of the imagination, but warmer. He crawled further in as he the lights in his head began to dim. "It'll make a good grave if nothing else," was his last conscious thought.

His primitive brain took over again, forcing his body further back into the small cave until it felt warmth. It snuggled his body up against the source of the warmth as his last, tiny vestiges of consciousness slipped away. Adrian was curled up against the rump of a hibernating pregnant bear. The fact that he had been eating absolutely nothing but bear meat and fat for weeks, had rubbed bear fat on his skin, was wearing a robe of bear hide, all made him smell like a bear. The smell of a human in that cave would have eventually awakened the bear; the smell that he exuded did not. Lying against the bear's rump warmed the only cool spot on the bear, making the bear more comfortable. The bear provided enough heat to keep Adrian alive. While he was unconscious and not moving, he was healing.

Outside the snow continued to fall, faster and thicker. Wolfgang found his dead hunter. He made the right decision and stayed on the frozen stream, heading downhill looking for tracks on either side. As the snow fell, his hopes fell with it. By the time he and his men passed the small overhang the snow was falling rapidly. Not one of the men glanced at the overhang; not one noticed it in any way. They walked on and eventually gave up, returning to camp defeated and exhausted. They barred themselves inside their cabins each night, and went into the woods as little as possible. They waited for the next attack. And waited.

Adrian was comatose for over a week without regaining consciousness, without dreams. When the swelling in his brain had retreated, he began to swim back to consciousness. The bear had shifted positions several times during the week, and Adrian had shifted with her. He was always against her rump, but sometimes it was his belly pressed up against it, and sometimes it was his back. At one point his arm had extended up over the sow and against her stomach. The twins inside were large now; they would be coming out soon. Spring was near. His hand felt the babies moving, his quiet subconscious brain had nothing better to do in the dark cave than to pay attention and observe, as it always did. The information was stored somewhere deep and inaccessible in Adrian's brain. Every bit of data in a man's brain helps to form who he is, and this was no exception.

When nearly ten days had passed, Adrian briefly came close to consciousness. On the eleventh day he came fully awake. He lay still for a long time gathering data. He was warm and it was almost pitch black. There was a small trickle of light coming from the direction of his feet. He was enveloped in a strong smell. A smell that normally he would have found overpowering, but because he had acclimated to it, wasn't. He slowly became aware that his face was pressed into something furry, the source of the warmth. It was something furry, warm, and very big. It was something alive. These thoughts were slow to form in his mind, awakening as it was from a long recovery.

His first coherent thought was, "Don't panic. Don't tense up, don't act awake. Don't panic." He lay still, gathering more data. He recalled with some difficulty that he had been head hit by a large caliber rifle bullet. He remembered vaguely killing the man who had shot him, although he wasn't clear on all of the details. He very vaguely recalled crawling into a hole under a tree.

"Oh Shit! I'm lying with my face on a bear that's asleep in a hole in the ground! Jesus Christ on little tiny crutches!" Adrian began to inch, ever so slowly, away from the bear. As he lost contact with its rump against his face the bear twitched, moved a bit, rumbled out a snore, and settled back to deep sleep. Adrian kept moving away slowly. As he crawled he found the rifle and brought it out with him.

When he crawled out of the hole into the blindingly bright sunlight bouncing off the untracked snow, he stumbled away from the hole two hundred yards then sat down to thank about what had happened, and what he had to do next. He had his hammer, still on his wrist with the thong. He had his bear robe, possibly a big part of why he hadn't awakened the bear and become her dinner. He had five pounds of bear pemmican. He was starving. He hadn't eaten in over a week and his body had used up a lot of energy healing and staying warm. He eagerly dug into the pemmican, but as he brought it up to his mouth the smell of it hit him hard. "What?" he thought. He had always loved the smell of the bear meat, loved the taste. But now he stared at it and threw it away. For some reason, he couldn't make himself eat it. Knew he would never eat bear meat again. "Strange."

He needed water, and found the canteen on his belt, but didn't recognize it. He didn't remember taking it from the dead man. The water inside was cold but not frozen. He drank it all, then put the canteen back on his belt. Now he needed food and shelter. He knew vaguely where he was. Knew that he had several food caches that he could get to, but they were all bear meat. He also needed to make another bow, or find the one he had lost. He had a lot to do before taking up the war again. He was ready to continue the assault on Wolfgang and his men, but an almost imperceptible tiny bit less eager. "First things first. Food, shelter, weapons, rest, finish healing. Then attack."

Adrian stood and moved back up the frozen creek. His legs were shaky but they steadied as he walked, warmed up, and stretched his cramped muscles. "Damn, saved by a sleeping bear. Who would believe that we hibernated together?" he mused to himself.

He reached the tree line again, found where he had killed the man. His "buddies" had left his body for the scavengers, and they had been at it pretty steady. Adrian probed around in the snow drift and found his bow, still in good shape thanks to the rawhide covering. He found the arrows too; they were slightly warped but could be straightened over a fire.

Adrian thought about where to take shelter and decided that his old wickiup would be ideal. "Far enough away they won't be looking for me. Close enough to get back when I'm ready to." He began walking east by south, taking care to cover his tracks where he could. When he got closer to his wickiup he began hunting elk. He was careful to watch for other elk hunters, a lesson he wouldn't soon forget. He hunted with the bow, using arrows with razor sharp flint points that he'd made what seemed like a long time ago, but had actually only been a few months. It didn't take him long to find and down an elk. He butchered and quartered the animal, then in six separate trips carried it to his wickiup.

A possum had taken up residence. He shooed it out, cleaned the place up, and soon had a cozy fire going. Adrian was ravenous, but possum was way down his list of potential meals. They were largely carrion eaters, essentially four legged vultures. Nothing he would eat unless he was far inside starvation's door. He stripped the elk down and began the process of making pemmican while eating as many fire-sizzled steaks as he could. He cooked marrowbones and sucked their rich and juicy insides. Roasted marrow was the tastiest thing in the wild world.

His body demanded redress for the near starvation he had put it through, and he gave it back as much as he could, as fast as he could. He slept from nightfall to daylight each day, often dreaming of bears. He was regaining his strength, building his food reserves and plotting his next moves. When he returned he would return with a vengeance. By now, Wolfgang must be hoping that the bullet had wounded and eventually killed him. He had been too quiet and left no tracks.

Adrian killed another elk and made the entire animal into pemmican. He used the hide to make par fleche bags to store it. A sharpened bone splinter from the elk made the needle which he used to sew them shut with strings of the elk's sinews. He ate everything else. Only the hooves and the bones were not completely used in one way or another. Even the bones were broken down and boiled after the marrow was removed. Boiling the bones removed the last traces of edible compounds inside the bone cells, making a thin but nutritious broth. A fine hot drink on cold days. The hooves could have been carved into ornaments. Adrian experimented with the broken bones and the hooves, making various arrow tips. He found ways to use them both, but not for the war.

The stick points with the slivers cut backwards in them were working fine, easy to make and maintain. "Don't over complicate," was a prime rule of combat. He began scouting out the enemy camp, as though it were the first time he had seen it. He suspected that they would have made some changes. He watched, waited, and watched some more. He only had a few weeks of snow to worry with. Soon it would begin to melt. With luck there might be one of those famous warm winds he remembered reading about in the western novels. "A sirocco? Something like that. A warm wind that melted off snow." When the snow was gone he would be free to move about as much as he wanted without leaving tracks. Then, the war would be on, really on.

CHAPTER 17

ADRIAN WATCHED THE CAMP FROM a new spot. He built a new low profile lean-to just tall enough for him to stretch out flat inside. It was shaped like a small pup-tent. He used forked sticks pushed into the ground, placing them in pairs at angles criss-crossing each other. Then he laid a long stick down the forks. This made a long and low A-frame structure. The space from the ground to the ridgepole spanned thirty inches. More sticks were laid against the ridgepole and tied off with cordage. Then he cut tree boughs and wove them in and out through the structure to hold them in place. He gathered dead grass, tied in bundles, and laid them over the boughs. When he was done, the lean-to blended in with its surroundings. It was built inside thick brush. It made a tube in which he could lay down full-length, and pull a brush plug into the opening if he wanted to block out the wind entirely. That was useful for when he slept in it at night. He added dead brush along it to break up any straight outlines.

His new shelter kept the snow from falling on him, and once covered with snow his body heat stayed inside with him. He covered the ground beneath him with pine boughs to create insulation between him and the cold, damp ground. He could stay there comfortably all day. All night too if he was inclined to. The camp was as it had been before. The morning trap patrol was still performed, but it was performed with a lack of enthusiasm. They had not found any new traps for a long time. But they would probably go on doing it until they knew for a fact that Adrian was dead.

The perimeter patrols performed their daily ritual as well. They still swept their trail every morning for new traps, and did not venture away from it. By now the swipe traps would be useless. The limbs, if still bent back, would have lost their ability to spring back. The punji pits could still be dangerous, but most likely they would be easy to spot now. The flimsy tops required maintenance or weather would collapse them. Adrian didn't think any of his traps would be of value now. It was time to put in some new ones, to let them know he was back. He watched carefully for three days and determined that there were new habits, new patterns he could use to his advantage.

The morning sweep was performed by the same men. They followed the same routine every time. They stood in the same place in line, started at the same places, stopped at the same places. It was like watching a clockwork machine. There were five places where they walked without checking the ground—short little areas where they transitioned from one sweep line to another. He took special note of those five places, visually counting off paces from various landmarks, cross referencing with paces from other land marks to exactly triangulate the spots. Then he went to sleep. He would be up all night so he would need the rest.

Sleep was something Adrian had almost always been able to do on a moment's notice. It was a skill he learned and perfected in the Army. A soldier sleeps when he can, and can sleep anywhere. Adrian had even learned to sleep while standing at attention in basic training. He, and most of the soldiers, could sleep for fifteen to twenty seconds while standing rigidly. During those seconds the soldier's body would begin to slowly move back and forth as it tried to keep its balance. Eventually the solider would lean too far, start to lose balance and snap back to attention. A platoon of men kept standing at attention for several hours looked like a forest of sea kelp slowly waving back and forth. Sleeping lying down in a snug, warm lean-to was a piece of cake, now that he had his war to distract him.

He waited until shortly after midnight. There were still no outside sentries, not after his hammer attack. He carefully located the five spots, dug in punji traps near each, and covered them. It took him until almost daylight. He had to be completely silent. If they knew he had been in camp that night they would be too careful when morning came. He thought he might get one man in one trap, if he was lucky. He exfiltrated the camp and returned to his lean-to. He waited as the sun came up and watched as the men came out and began to perform their exact routine. They missed stepping in his first trap by inches, missed the second trap by at least a foot.

Their blind luck ended when one of the men stepped into the third trap and screamed. His scream was of rage, not pain. He would lose the foot, become one of the cooks, one of the cripples that remained always in camp, invisible to the two-footed men. That is, if he survived the crude amputation he was about to experience, and weeks of painful healing. His outrage was palpable. The rest of the men froze in their tracks. No one moved to help him for a solid minute. Then the men began using the sticks with true intensity, the way they should have been using them, but had been lulled away from in Adrian's absence. It didn't take them long to find the other four traps. During the search the men were constantly making obscene gestures towards the wood line, once or twice in his actual direction. Their terror and anger had been rekindled. If they ever caught him alive they would torture him for weeks before letting him die.

Adrian watched. He didn't feel the same exhilaration that he had felt before the head wound. He didn't feel remorse; the war was still on and they had started it. They were the lowest form of human life imaginable—cannibals. He only felt grim satisfaction in a plan that worked. He continued to watch as the men completed sweeping the camp for traps, and then as the roving patrols moved carefully out to do their rounds. They swept everything in front of them all the way to their usual trails, then swept those thoroughly, too. Adrian knew they would after finding fresh traps in camp. It was pointless to have set traps for them, so he hadn't. He had planted the traps in their minds now, a far more effective strategy.

Adrian had maintained a count of how many men were able-bodied. His attacks had taken a large toll on Wolfgang's force. Wolfgang did not have a source from which he could draw more recruits. Every man lost was a drop in resources. They had gotten better at treating the wounds he and his traps inflicted. They had learned the hard way that the only chance to save the men was to completely carve out all tissue around the wound to its full diameter, then cauterize the entire area with white-hot metal rods. He had seen them perform the operation four times, each time outside on one of the picnic tables. They learned to do it as soon as the wounded man was back in camp. It was a gruesome sight to see. Each time they did it, the man's life had been saved, but usually at the cost of the full use of his body. Doing that to a shoulder wound pretty much guaranteed that arm wouldn't work again. A wound in the thigh and the leg was never strong again.

Whenever he watched this procedure it had disappointed him that the men would be spared. He would have to kill them at some point. He also noticed how agitated the rest of the men became. They would prowl the camp restlessly, looking at the woods with angry faces. Psychologically these men were at their wits' end. They didn't know what to do about Adrian. They had tried as hard as they knew how to find him, and had only gotten men killed in the process. He came into their camp at night with impunity, seemingly invisible. They only felt safe at night, barred inside their cabins, and even then they were scared to death of him setting the cabins on fire. They wondered why he didn't. During the day they were safe as long as they stayed in camp. Safe, so far. They knew that he had rifles and ammunition. If he chose to start sniping they wouldn't be safe anywhere. They wondered why he didn't.

Adrian knew the usefulness of the poisoned puncture wound had run its course. It was time to change tactics. It was time to shake up the game, come at them from a completely new angle. Adrian gave it a lot of thought, decided that he would wait for his next moves until after the snow melt. That should only be two or three weeks at most. Spring was well underway. Plants were growing again. Adrian's war could wait. He was in no hurry, had no plans to go anywhere. He had no plans for after the war. He was a patient man with an obsession. He would check back in on them every few days. Leave them some sign that he was still around to keep them on their toes.

Adrian returned to his wickiup camp and made some minor improvements. He re-mudded the interior and refreshed the brush covering on the exterior. He sewed up some new holes in the hides that covered it—mice had been eating while he was away. He was keeping his hands busy while his mind worked on his next set of tactics. After four days he decided to return and leave a few fresh traps in the roving patrols corridor. He knew they would find them, but that was OK. They were just to let them know he was still around. As he approached the camp he walked parallel to the east footpath. He noticed something new. On the path there was a signpost, and a sign.

"Ah, he thought. "Bait! They're trying to get me to come to the sign to read it. Either they have an ambush set up, or they have rigged their own traps. If it was me I would set the trap for the furthest spot from which the sign can be seen and read. Not right in front of it."

Adrian sat down and waited until dark. He knew that if there were men waiting in ambush that they would give themselves away. Men are restless creatures, sooner or later they have to move or talk. The battle of ambush goes to the one who can wait the longest without moving. If they had seen Adrian they would have already attacked, so he simply sat down where he was and waited. After the night was half over and he had not heard or seen a sign of a human, he was convinced there was no ambush. It was too dark to look for traps, so he lay down and went to sleep.

At daylight he ate a double handful of elk pemmican. It wasn't as good as the bear pemmican had been, not as rich, but he still had absolutely no interest in eating bear meat. Elk pemmican would do the job. He waited to see if perhaps men would come to set up an ambush, but none showed. He slowly checked out the area he thought would be most likely to be booby-trapped but found nothing. He stood and read the sign from forty yards away. It was plain and simple, and a complete game-changer. Adrian was stunned by the simplicity of it, the evil genius of it. Wolfgang's checkmate took him completely by surprise.

Adrian slowly moved away from the area of the sign. He circled the camp and found three more in obvious locations. Wolfgang wanted Adrian to know. He had made sure that Adrian would see one of the signs. He worked himself carefully into a position where he could observe. He would confirm with his own eyes that Wolfgang was telling the truth. Wolfgang was.

CHAPTER 18

ADRIAN WATCHED THE HOSTAGES HELD in the picnic table shelter. He could see four women, two children—a boy and a girl—and two men. They were not tied, but they were guarded by four armed men. They weren't going to escape. As he watched, they were put to work cooking lunch. They were roasting meat over the large, open grill. Wolfgang's men would come in and eat on a shift schedule. Ten men at a time only. They leered at the women as they ate. It was easy to see, even from the distance Adrian watched, that these men were hungry for women. From what his nailed-to-the-wall prisoner had told him, when they did get their hands on women, it was gang rape, sometimes to the death. What his prisoner hadn't told him but he now knew, was that the victims would be eaten afterwards.

Adrian dimly recalled having seen some of these hostages in the village—a lifetime ago, when he first came to the mountains. He had watched the village from hiding, decided he didn't want to talk to anyone, and moved on. He had made no contact with them, or anyone else, since leaving the Palo Duro Canyon. Wolfgang had out-thought him that was for sure. Adrian had watched the village, and a couple of small tribes as well. There were other people on the mountain besides Wolfgang and his men, but Adrian had largely forgotten about them, until now. He was only reminded of them when the hunters returned with "meat."

The sign had said, "Adrian—what you do to us, we do to the hostages." So simple, so irreversibly game-changing. It had returned Adrian to sanity in one long dizzying moment. Wolfgang had ended Adrian's personal war completely with that one simple move. Adrian's head was spinning with the implications. He had never considered that the village was in play. He had barely thought about it at all, seeing it as just something that might move Wolfgang to leave camp, creating opportunities for ambush along the road. If Adrian *had* thought of Wolfgang taking hostages to use against him, he might have dismissed it. What did he care what happened to the villagers? It wasn't his village, he didn't know those people. He didn't owe them anything. If they got captured it was their own fault for being weak and stupid. The village should have eradicated Wolfgang and his thugs a long time ago. But seeing the hostages was different.

He didn't understand the village's apparent weakness. There were enough of them to put up a good fight. He had seen guns; surely there were many more that he hadn't seen. There weren't as many men in the village as Wolfgang had, but there were enough to fight. Enough to make sure Wolfgang would leave them alone afterward. They had families to defend—why on earth had they not done something about these criminals a long time ago? Why tolerate the "protection" costs? Adrian was incapable of bending his mind to a point of view that made acceptance of tyranny palatable. He would die first; he didn't understand anyone thinking otherwise.

But when he saw the hostages, he knew his personal war was over. These were innocent people involuntarily drawn into his war. He would not, under any circumstances, be the direct cause of harm to these people. Not if he could help it. This was no longer about him. It was no longer a matter in which time was on his side. Time was against him now. Sooner or later, Wolfgang would allow the men to rape the women, and children. No doubt the men too. Sooner or later Wolfgang would demand Adrian's surrender, and start killing hostages on a timetable until he did. Adrian had one big card to buy time with: to avoid letting Wolfgang know he was aware of the hostage situation. He had to leave no sign he was anywhere in the vicinity. He had to change his strategy; the tactics would follow.

If Wolfgang got even a whiff that Adrian had read the sign and seen the hostages, he would immediately start hurting them to bring Adrian in. He wouldn't be satisfied to simply use the threat of harming them as a shield, he would actively harm them, even kill them, to get Adrian in his clutches. There was no way that Wolfgang would allow Adrian to walk away. He wanted to kill Adrian in the worst possible kind of way, literally. Adrian had been routinely insulting Wolfgang for so long that hatred consumed every waking second of Wolfgang's life.

It was still war, but it was no longer just Adrian's war. It was the villagers' war too. Adrian had to go to the village, face their wrath for having given the raiders an excuse to take hostages, then convince them to fight with him, or continue to be slaves. He would have to be convincing. He might get shot before he even had a chance to convince them. Surely they would take out their anger on him, since they didn't seem to be taking it out on Wolfgang. Adrian viewed the villagers as weak, or they would have done something about Wolfgang a long time ago.

Weak people, Adrian thought, invariably directed their anger at the wrong target. They defended themselves in their own minds, gave themselves excuses. They misdirected their own thoughts away from rightfully blaming themselves by wrongfully blaming others, or circumstances they thought were beyond their control. Adrian believed he would walk into a group of weak willed people, and that instead of laying blame where it belonged just might lay it on him since he was only one man. After all, they would be able to gang up on one man, giving themselves an outlet for the anger that should be directed at themselves for allowing the situation to continue, and Wolfgang for causing the whole thing in the first place.

Adrian left the camp and walked back to his wickiup. He was careful not to leave tracks. If he had been Wolfgang he would have sent out three-man patrols to roam the mountainside at random, looking for signs and tracks. Wolfgang had surprised him with the hostage move; perhaps he was smarter than Adrian had given him credit for. Perhaps he just thought differently, which was almost the same thing, and often had the same result. The random patrols might be out; it would be a good move. It was a simple tactic. They didn't know where Adrian was; only that he was drawn over and over to the mining camp. It was a statistical thing. Send out patrols, have them roam around in a large circle around the camp. Allow them to choose when and in what direction to move. Tell them to stop frequently, spend a whole day where they thought he might appear. Sooner or later the math would work out and they would spot him.

Adrian was cautious, frequently checking all around him for signs of stalkers. He watched and listened to the wildlife. A bird suddenly flying up, or turning sharply away at the last second before landing in a bush, could indicate a hidden watcher, man or beast. Birds were one of the best signals that something was different in an area. There were other signals. Squirrels would fuss, or suddenly stop chucking to the other squirrels. A frightened squirrel running up a tree made a distinctive sound as its claws dug into the bark. Startled deer would snort, a short, loud exhalation of air through the nostrils. Often they would stamp their feet several times. When deer or elk ran, they could be heard for a long time as they tore up the ground, long after they had vanished from sight. Crows and magpies would sound the alarm when seeing a stranger. Adrian listened for these audible signals, and was careful to not cause them himself so that someone else might hear.

He stopped to listen often. He listened for silence where there should be background noises indicating someone or something that didn't belong. Tree frogs suddenly going silent, bird sounds conspicuously absent. He listened closely, for lack of sounds were as telling as sounds themselves. He used his sense of smell as much as he could. Some odors could be easily detected by a man. Men living in the woods often stank, smelling of stale sweat, unclean habits, and smoke from sitting by many fires. In the right conditions they could be located two or three hundred yards away. Adrian walked slowly, carefully, leaving as few tracks as possible, all the while sniffing silently at the air.

He took the necessary amount of time, but moved as

quickly as he could under the circumstances. He couldn't afford to slip up now and get captured or killed. It would be easy to become overly hasty and under-cautious. It was necessary to take precautions, and those precautions took time to implement. Time was no longer on his side. He had gone from a relaxed state of mind to a man driven by an immutable deadline, only he didn't know what the deadline was. He just knew there was one, and people's lives depended on him beating it. "Deadline—truer nomenclature there never was," he thought.

He wasn't looking forward to the scene he was likely to encounter at the village, but he had to go. He had to recruit them into the war. The war had changed. Now it needed to be fought and ended as soon as possible. All of Wolfgang's men, and especially Wolfgang himself, had to be killed. They were a cancerous growth that the people of the mountain could no longer tolerate. They had to do something about it. They had to help—their people had been taken hostage. He had to get through to them quickly, move them past what he expected to be their anger at him, and get them motivated toward the right and proper goal.

Adrian saw the village, waited in the woods, and watched for a few minutes. He looked down at himself and thought about the impression he was about to make. He had stopped at a creek that had a pool of unfrozen water. Spring really was close. He had bathed, cut his hair, and shaved, using his surgically sharp bowie knife. He had put the Stone Age tools away. He had left his hammer and flint tools in his wickiup. He replaced them with the modern steel knife, rifle, and pistol. He dressed in his best elk skin clothes, cleaning them as well as possible short of washing them. There was no time for washing and drying leather clothes, not in this weather. They would see a wild man. Tall and thin, but not unhealthily so. His hair was cut short, but done so seemingly randomly; it was difficult to give oneself a decent haircut with a large knife. He was gaunt and his skin was pale white from the long winter. Scars from the bear's claws showed above his collar, long, puckered, and red furrows that went down his chest and arm. He hadn't spoken aloud in months, and when he tried out his voice it out had sounded strange to him. It was croaky from lack of use. He would not make much of an impression on these people. He had been living like a Stone Age man for a long time, and it showed.

"Nothing for it, just do it and get on with the show," he thought as he stepped onto the main road into the village and walked into sight. He didn't know what to expect, but he was certain it would be unpleasant. He walked into the village, stopped in the street and stood there looking around. There was no one in sight. All the buildings were shuttered and doors closed. There was smoke coming from some of the chimneys. People were in the buildings, waiting for something or someone whom was most certainly not welcome. It was a pleasant enough day, people would normally be outside on a day like this. Adrian stood there for what seemed ages, then a door slowly opened. Adrian thought, "OK, here we go. Bad stuff about to happen."

Adrian called out loudly, but just short of a shout. "Hello, I'm Adrian Hunter. I need to talk to the village leader."

What happened next was beyond anything Adrian had imagined.

CHAPTER 19

AN OLDER WOMAN STEPPED OUT of the doorway that had opened. Other doors opened up one after another up and down the street. Armed men, and in some cases armed women, stepped out of the doorways. "Uh-oh," Adrian thought. "This is going to get ugly fast." But he needed to enlist their aid, so he stood his ground. The armed people were soon joined by others, some armed some not. Children came out too. They all stared at Adrian with expressions that were impossible to read.

The old woman said, "Adrian Hunter, you said? You the Adrian Hunter what's been warring on Wolfgang?" She stepped closer, scrutinizing Adrian up and down.

Adrian asked with puzzlement "Yes, Ma'am. How did you know about that?"

The old woman grinned and strode up to Adrian with her hand out to shake. "Why son, you're a legend all up and down these mountains and probably across half the entire United States by now, or what's left of it. We heard about you from that deserter that run away from Wolfgang. We caught him skulking around here and he told us all about how you was whupping those boys up there on the mountain all by yourself. You're a hero, son, a gol-darned gold-plated honest-to-God hero round here." The old woman pumped Adrian's hand up and down like she was never going to stop.

People were crowding all around him, slapping him on the back, their faces filled with smiles. The children were fighting to get to a spot where they could reach out and touch him. Adrian was frozen in shock. He didn't know what to do; he was starting to feel panicky with so many people crowded up against him.

"Whoa now!" the old woman shouted. "Whoa now! Give the boy room to breathe. Good God, folks, back up! Don't trample him. We want him to feel welcome don't we? Give him some room I said!" The old woman began pushing people back, clearing a small space in front of them. She turned back to Adrian and said, "Son, we've been praying you'd come along here someday. We need your help. Come along with me to the meeting room, we need to get everyone together." The old woman turned and walked off. Adrian, still too shocked to say anything, automatically followed. The entire crowd followed on his heels.

Adrian entered the room behind the old woman. The rest of the village crowded in. The room filled with men, women, and children. There was jostling as the villagers jockeyed to get in position to see Adrian. They kept a small distance from him, but he was feeling claustrophobic in the crowded room filled with strangers who seemed to be in awe of him. "Like a visiting movie star," Adrian thought. Two old men joined the old woman at the front of the room. She grabbed up a gavel lying on a trestle table and began banging the tabletop. "Quiet, everybody, quiet. We have town business to discuss and not much time to do it in. Quiet now, quiet!" She banged the gavel lighter and lighter and the murmuring of the crowd settled into an intense silence.

The three elders took seats behind the table, facing Adrian and the crowd. The old woman said, "Somebody fetch him a chair. Don't make him stand there! Come on, move it! Hurry up and bring him a chair." A chair appeared in the back of the room and was handed overhead from hand to hand until it reached Adrian. He took the chair and sat down at the head of the table. He didn't know whether to look at the elders or at the villagers, so he sat at an angle where he could see both.

The old woman stood up. "Ladies and Gentlemen, as you have no doubt heard by now, this is Adrian Hunter!" She pointed at Adrian with a dramatic gesture as she spoke. The villagers began shouting and whistling, stomping their feet and clapping. Some of the women were crying, some of the men were laughing. Adrian thought they had gone nuts. He was trapped in a room with a bunch of crazies. He had expected bad things when he came to the village, but this was crazy.

The old woman began pounding the gavel again. She was quite a showman, controlling the crowd easily. She got them to silence again, and when the room was quiet she turned to Adrian and said, "Tell us what to do. Show us how to get our people back and how to get rid of those monsters once and for all. Tell us, son, we've been waiting for you. The floor is yours." The old woman sat down with a sigh of pure relief, as though she had just set down the heaviest burden that a woman could bear. The villagers looked at Adrian with fascinated anticipation.

Adrian thought, "They look at me like gold and pearls

are about to spew out of my mouth. Too bad it won't happen that way, but I'll make the best of it." He stood and faced the villagers.

"I saw the hostages this morning. They were in good physical condition at the time. I don't think that will last long, though. We have two enemies, time and Wolfgang, in that order. If you're willing to go to battle for your people, if you're willing to fight for your homes and your families, I'll lead you. If you do exactly what I tell you to do, when I tell you to do it, you can win and rid yourselves of those cannibals. You can get your people back and you can kill every one of those sons-of-bitches."

The villagers cheered, shouted, clapped, whistled, stomped, and waved their arms like nothing he had ever seen before. "My God!" he thought. "They would follow me into a lion's den armed with switches. If they hold on to that enthusiasm, we have a real shot at this." Adrian held up his arms to quiet them and the crowd went silent instantly. "Folks, we have to move fast. We need every able-bodied man that can walk and shoot. No children and no women. Men eighteen years or older only. Meet me in the street in thirty minutes. Bring your best rifles and pistols. Bring shotguns if you can carry them, too. Dress warm. Bring whatever you can to eat. There won't be any fires for cooking, so bring food you can eat cold. We'll need drinking water and bed rolls, too. Wear clothes that blend in, nothing white or brightly colored. Your best walking boots or shoes. Hurry up, let's move. Outside this door in thirty minutes. Go!"

Adrian sat back down as the room quickly emptied. "What's going on? If they're so eager to fight, why haven't they already attacked?" Adrian asked the old woman.

"They want to fight but they don't know how. There

isn't a military background in the entire village. This village was set up twenty years ago as a self-sustaining pacifist farming community. No fighters. The guns we have were for hunting. We lived by a strict pacifist code, kept ourselves separated from the rest of the world—it had become too evil to bear. Pacifism works when there are rules of law, and people willing to enforce those rules with whatever force is required. But we have discovered that in a world without rule of law, pacifism is suicidal. Pacifists too easily become victims, basically begging to be run over. We've talked and talked about it. All we know to do would be to walk up the road and start shooting. That probably wouldn't work out so well. We were on the verge of doing just that when you showed up.

"Used to be all Wolfgang did was come in with about twenty armed men and tell us to bring them food. We would pile the food up until they were satisfied and left. We still had enough to get by. A gunfight right here in our streets didn't seem wise. When we heard about you, and how you were whipping up on them single-handed, it was like a miracle. One man could do that? If one man could do that, imagine what we could do if we just knew how. We kept hoping you'd come see us, come lead us. When they took our people hostage, it changed. We knew we had to do something, but we still didn't know how to go about it. We simply don't know what to do, where to go, how to attack. Their fighting men out number our fighting men, so a straight up attack didn't seem the right way to do it. Yet what else could we do? We couldn't figure out anything, though. No expertise. When you showed up today it was the most perfect timing you could ever imagine. We were going to march up the road tomorrow and probably commit suicide. But now, now you can lead us. You can show us what to do, and how to do it."

Adrian sat quietly for a moment. "How many able-bodied men will I have to work with?"

"Twenty three men over 18 years of age. Armed with every kind of rifle you can imagine. All the willingness you could dream of, but no fighting skills. Enthusiasm galore and guts too. But no idea what to do, or how to do it."

"Twenty three'll be enough. I have a plan in mind and they should be able to execute it. I'll need to get them out of town and into the woods before I explain the plan. I don't want anyone here in the village to know what we're going to do. If Wolfgang sends men here to grab more hostages or to interrogate I don't want him forewarned. He'd find out we're out there planning an attack—which is bad enough—but he won't know the exact plan. I won't tell the men the key details until the last moment. We're outnumbered and our attack depends on surprise. If Wolfgang knew our plan he could come up with a way to defend himself and his men against it. You spread the word to the people who stay behind. They must not say anything to anyone. Secrecy is absolutely imperative. If they talk, they may end up bringing down the whole thing, which in this case, would mean the end of this village."

The old woman asked, "Is it true what that man told us? Did you kill twenty of Wolfgang's men with a bow and arrow? You've been fighting them by yourself all winter? They haven't been down to bother us. Did you have them so scared that they wouldn't leave camp?"

Adrian replied, "I hate to count the dead like that, but it was more than twenty, and more put out of action permanently. I let them leave camp to hunt for food, so they wouldn't need to raid your village any sooner than necessary. Other than that I kept them pretty much bottled up most of the time. It's not as hard as you might imagine, if you've had the training and experience that I've had."

The old woman said "More than twenty? Damn it, son, you must be a holy terror on wheels. Do you have any idea how far and wide your story has been told? People out there are desperate for good news. They are desperate for leadership. There are too many bad guys out there, and not enough good guys. They talk about you around campfires at night. Stories are told about you that couldn't possibly be true. It's like Daniel Boone or Davie Crockett all over again. You're a legend, and that legend is going to grow and grow with each retelling. I've even heard the stories being told on the ham radio—it's spread everywhere. People need a hero, and it looks like you stepped up at the right time and in the right way to fill that role."

"That can't be," Adrian said. "I haven't done that much, and it wasn't that hard. They made me mad, really mad. So I decided to take them to task for it, and I have. But it isn't something that proves leadership. What I've been doing isn't enviable, shouldn't be something to hold up as an example. I have been killing men in the meanest way possible. How is that heroic?"

The old woman said, "Son, you don't understand. Those men deserve every misery you put on them and then some; and everyone damn well knows it. There are other groups like them that deserve it too, and other people that would love to see you come do it, or to help them do it. If nothing else, it gives them hope that maybe they can do it themselves. People need heroes, especially in this day and age. Say, those are some pretty nasty scars. What got hold of you? Was it something Wolfgang's men did?"

"These? No, I ran into a grizzly bear and we got into a fight. I killed him with my spear, but it was a close thing." The old woman slapped her knee and laughed a high old woman's cackle. "See there! That's what I'm talkin' about. You killed a grizzly bear with a sharp stick and act like it was nothing special. From the spread of his claws he was a monster bear! I'll tell that story tonight. In a week it will have traveled far out onto the plains and over the mountains to the coast. It'll be picked up on the ham radio and spread like wildfire. People will add it to the legend, how Hunter killed a grizzly bear with a stick. The campfires will be resounding with tales, taller and taller every day. You're a natural son, a natural."

Adrian heard the buzzing sound of men gathering outside. He got up, shook his head with dismay at the old woman, knowing nothing he could say would stop her from making a big deal out of the bear story. He walked outside and saw that most of the men were there, a few more trotting down the street. He counted heads. Twenty-three, just like the old woman said. She knew her people, she was a natural politician. Adrian was afraid she would make a career out of pumping up those Hunter stories. Nothing he could do about it right now. There were bigger fish to fry.

"Listen up. We're going into the woods. When we get away from here I'll tell you the plan, explain it so that each of you understands your part in it." Adrian turned and walked up the street towards the forest.

The ragged band of men followed behind him, cheering and chanting. "Hunter! Hunter! Hunter!" turning his name into a war chant. They followed the elk skin-clad tall man as he strode rapidly and confidently into the dark woods. They were on their way to give hell to their enemies, at long last.

CHAPTER 20

H E STOPPED IN A SMALL clearing a half-mile into the woods, and turned to face the twenty-three men following him. "Men, I have a small speech to make. Settle down and get comfortable." He waited while they sorted themselves out, dropping packs and squatting on their heels or sitting on the ground. When they had settled in he said, "This is a volunteer mission. I don't know you men; I don't know what each of you is capable of or not capable of. I don't have time to find out the right way, either. Normally I'd want a full month with you before starting what we are going to do, but we don't have that luxury. So, I have to depend on you to be honest, not just with me, but with yourself, and your neighbor next to you.

"I know each and every one of you wants to help and is willing to fight. At least in the heat of the moment you believe you are. It's easy to get caught up in all the hoorah, to get snarled up in peer pressure. But there are men who aren't made for fighting, and if they try, they get themselves and others hurt or killed. There is no shame or embarrassment attached to that. We're not all built alike. I can't play a guitar, tried to but couldn't get the feel of the thing. There is no shame in that. It's just the nature of man that some are fighters and some aren't. Some are painters and some aren't. Each of you are to take a half hour to sit quietly and think about this. Are you sure you can fight? Are you sure that when the lead starts flying, you can shoot back, and actually aim to kill a man? Are you sure that if the man standing next to you catches a bullet in the face that you can keep on going into those bullets? These are hard questions. Tough questions. I don't expect every one of you to say you can.

"I'm going to the other side of the meadow, and I'll wait there. In half an hour I want those who truly believe they can fight to come to me, one at a time. I want you to come over there and look me straight in the eyes and tell me that you can fight. I want you to give me your personal word of honor that you will fight to the death if need be. I want your oath that you will die for the man standing next to you and for the people behind you in the village. I also want your sworn word that you will follow my orders instantly and without question. That, too, is of extraordinary importance. I might give you orders that you believe in your own heart to be wrong, or incorrect for the situation. But obedience is the essence of discipline and discipline wins wars more than anything else.

"Any man that can't honestly do that should go back to the village and defend it. In my eyes you will be every bit a man as the ones who say they can fight. Defending the village is just as important as what we are going to do. Any man that can look into his own soul and see the truth, and act appropriately on that truth, is a man to respect, and will always have my respect." Adrian walked across the meadow and sat with his back to the group. He took out his bowie knife and began sharpening it, even though it didn't need sharpening. He was nervous, afraid that maybe his speech was too convincing, that none of the men would follow him now.

Thirty minutes later the men lined up and began walking across the meadow to Adrian one at a time, each taking a moment to look directly into his eyes and swear an oath in their own words to follow his orders and fight to the death for his comrades. It took an hour for all twenty-three men to swear their oaths. Adrian could not have been happier with the results. These men had taken his speech to heart. They had looked at him with clear eyes and clean consciences and sworn their allegiance to him. They would fight as well as they knew how, and they would obey his orders. It was up to him to use them efficiently, to not waste their efforts or their loyalties—or their lives.

When all of the men were sworn in, Adrian addressed them again. "OK, we need to elect officers. You men know each other and have some idea of each other's capabilities. We need four captains. I'm going to break you up into four groups of six, with one five-man group that I'll lead myself. Normally I select the captains. But, we don't have time for me to get to know everyone that well, so I am depending on you. No false modesty, please; it will only get people killed. No personal animosities. Just honest evaluations as to who are the four best leaders in this group. We will do it by secret ballot.

"Anyone have paper and a pencil? All right, hand out pieces of paper big enough to write four names. Pass them out. Each of you write down the four names of the men you think should be captains. Go with your instincts; don't over-think it. You already know in your gut who they are so let your gut tell you. Don't show them to each other. Don't discuss your choices. Write them down, fold them over, and hand them to me. Nominate yourself if you think you should. Hurry up now."

Ten minutes later Adrian had counted the votes. "The Captains are, and by almost unanimous votes, Jeff, Charles, George and Kyle. You men step forward, let me see who you are." The four men stepped forward almost shyly, yet with evident pride in having been chosen. Each told Adrian his name.

Adrian announced, "Now Captains, it's time to choose the men for your group, here's how you do it. I'll choose the men and send them to you. If I send you someone that you have personal problems with, problems that you believe will interfere with performing your duties, send him back to me. But only do so if you are sure you and he can't work together. Same goes for you men, when I send you to your Captain. If you have a problem with that Captain, let me know. We don't have time to do this any other way, so make sure it's a real problem that will really interfere, not some petty squabble."

Adrian then assigned the men to the four Captains. He chose by age and fitness level, equalizing the teams. There were no kickbacks from either end. "Good. OK, men, gather round." The men seated themselves in a semi-circle in front of Adrian. He was pleased to see that they naturally separated into their four groups. "Captains, think about the men assigned to you and choose a lieutenant from your group. Your lieutenant will act in your absence, carry out assigned missions, and take your place if you are disabled or killed. Choose as well as you can.

We have two missions. First, we rescue the hostages.

Second, we go to war. Do not confuse the two in your minds. Our first mission is to get the hostages out of there and safely back home. Your assignments will require strict mission discipline. If, in the process of freeing the hostages, you see an opportunity to kill enemies, don't do it unless it will help us in the rescue operation. Do not stray from the mission. It is one of the worst mistakes you can make. It is one of the easiest mistakes to make. Amateurs make that mistake. The mission objective is the one and only thing you are to achieve. Nothing else matters. Nothing else counts. Anything else is a distraction and lessens the chances of achieving the objective. I cannot stress this enough—do you understand?"

He was met with vague head nodding and a couple of thumbs up. Adrian jumped to his feet and, putting on his best drill sergeant imitation, screamed at the men, "I said do you understand! Don't give me a goofy fucking nod or stupid thumbs up! You yell your answer! Now—DO YOU UNDERSTAND?"

The men all jumped to their feet yelling, "Yes Sir!"

Adrian said loudly, "You sound like you're not sure. Let me repeat. The mission objective is everything. Only a stupid idiot wandering around with his head up his ass forgets what the objective is and does something else, and if that happens, the mission will FAIL! DO YOU UNDERSTAND ME?"

"YES SIR!" they all shouted, making the forest ring.

Adrian shouted back, "Do you think you can all say it at the same time? Do you?

"YES SIR!" they all shouted, closer to being in unison.

"Once more, damnit—you're supposed to be a fighting unit. At least sound like one. All together now. The mission objective is the only thing you need to concern yourself with. DO YOU UNDERSTAND?"

"YES SIR!" they shouted in unison this time.

"Very good. Captains, get your men together. We have several miles to cover. Everyone in single-file. Maintain ten feet distance between each man. We're going to do some cover drills along the way. At random times I'll shout or signal 'cover' and I want every man to hit the dirt on opposite sides of the trail, flat on their bellies, behind any cover available, rifles pointing out. This has to become an automatic response. I'll also use the following hand signals. I want you to get used to them; obedience has to be automatic and instant."

Adrian showed them four hand signals. One for stop, one for stop and cover, one for silence, and one for follow. "We only have a few hours to learn what normally takes months. Pay close attention; don't let your minds wander. OK, follow me, single-file, ten-foot intervals, absolutely no talking."

With that, he moved into the woods. As soon as the men were strung out behind him he hit them with the stop and cover signal. There was a slow ragged response. Adrian strode up and down the line, showing each man how he should be positioned; making sure each man's rifle was pointed in the correct direction. He used positive encouragement. Explained it all again individually. Then as soon as they were moving and strung out he did it again. And again. And again. But now, each Captain was able to correct his own men. It took two hours to cover a half mile, but by the end of it the men were reacting to his signals like old professionals. It was a good enough start.

Adrian led the men towards the mining camp. When they were within a quarter-mile he gathered the men together. The way they gathered in their respective units was encouraging. "I'm going to take the four Captains with me from here. We are going to infiltrate the edge of the camp so that they can see where the buildings are, where the sentries are posted, and where the hostages are being held. I can't take all of you—it would be too risky. When we come back I'll draw a map and explain the operation. While we are gone, Lieutenants, check your men's weapons and ammunition. Make sure all weapons are ready and loaded. Have extra ammunition handy, but make sure it's secured and won't fall out when running or taking cover. Have every man jump up and down and listen for any jangling sounds, then find a way to silence it. Maintain absolute silence. No unnecessary talking, no walking around. Stay low and stay quiet. Wolfgang has patrols out, so don't draw their attention or it'll blow the mission. Stow all of your gear here except for weapons."

Adrian led the four men to a good vantage point at the edge of the forest. He explained about the roving patrol, where they would be, and how to avoid them. They crawled into position and Adrian whispered as he pointed out the various buildings and terrain features. The hostages were in the picnic building, cooking dinner. It would be dark in a few hours. They would have to move fast if they were going to pull off this operation today. Waiting for tomorrow wasn't an option; Wolfgang could lose his patience at any time.

As they watched, Wolfgang came out of his cabin, strode up to the hostages, and began yelling at them. He groped one of the younger women and viciously backhanded one of the men that tried to interfere, knocking him unconscious. It was plain that at least one of the women would be raped that night. One of Adrian's Captains stiffened and acted as though he might jump

175

up and rush down to the scene. He didn't, but it was obvious that he was closely related in some way to the woman or the man. Adrian didn't ask. In a village that small he assumed that all of his men were closely related to one or more of the hostages. Motivating his men wasn't an issue. Not knowing their capabilities, and their inexperience fighting, especially the fact that they had never fought together—those were the issues. He moved back and the Captains moved back with him.

"I'm going to kill the roving guards," Adrian said. "You four go back and tell the men to get ready. I'll only be a few minutes."

"Alone, General Hunter?" Kyle asked. "You're going to kill four men by yourself, and it's only going to take you a few minutes? "

The way Kyle asked made Adrian realize that what to him was a simple chore was an impossibly extraordinary feat to these men. He also noticed that he had been promoted to General. His men back at Fort Brazos would laugh their asses off at that.

"Kyle, I've watched these men for weeks. I know where they are right now and I know exactly where they'll be in ten minutes. I know this forest so well I can run through it at full speed in pitch dark, and have. I've had years of training in close quarter combat fighting, and more years than that actually doing it. In short, I'm an expert at this. It's no big thing, believe it or not. I'll meet up with you before you know it. Now go, but be quiet and don't be seen."

Adrian turned and melted into the forest as the four men watched. The next few hours would change their lives forever.

CHAPTER 21

"**G**ENERAL HUNTER—GOOD LORD!" ADRIAN THOUGHT. He couldn't help a small grin while shaking his head at the thought of it. He heard the roving patrol coming along right on schedule. "Creatures of habit. Well that habit ends in a few seconds."

He had hidden immediately next to the trail at the point where the two sets of guards would come together briefly as they circled the camp in opposite directions. They had made the trip around the camp about a thousand times by now, and were bored to the point of blindness. Adrian was well hidden and these men weren't looking anymore. As they came together they paused for a moment and Adrian launched out of the brush, bowie knife in hand. He ripped open the throat of the closest man with a forward slash of his knife. He pushed his way into the group men and slashed the second man's throat with a backhand as he brought the knife back. Two men down before they had time to react.

He shoved the body of the second man into the third and fourth men to knock them off balance, stopping them from removing their shoulder-slung rifles and firing off a warning shot. The impact from the thrown guard knocked them backward and they stumbled to the ground, their arms occupied trying to push off the body and keep their balance. He jumped on top of them, slashed and stabbed with his knife, the blade a blur of motion. Adrian stood and double-checked the men were dead or would soon be, and couldn't give warning. He collected their weapons and ammunition. Their rifles and pistols were better than what some of his men had and would be gladly received.

Adrian was a few minutes behind the Captains when he walked into the temporary camp. He had been able to move through the forest faster because he knew it well, and nearly caught up to them. Kyle was telling the men what "General Hunter" had said he was going to do when Adrian walked up, splattered with blood and carrying extra rifles, pistols and ammunition. The men gawked, some with their mouths hanging open. Adrian pretended not to notice. These men were simply too easily impressed, yet it solidified his position as the one with expertise and gave them more confidence. His own men back at Fort Brazos wouldn't have given him a second look; any of them could have done the same thing with the same ease.

"Gather round, men." Adrian cleared the leaves away from an area and using a twig began drawing out a map of the camp, pointing out the different cabins and features. The Captains, having just seen the camp, nodded with understanding.

"Here's the plan." Adrian began outlining what each group would do, when they would do it, and how they would do it. He talked steadily for fifteen minutes. Then he repeated the whole thing from the beginning, asking for any questions along the way. He reminded them of the old booby traps he had set in the area. "I don't think any of the swipes will work now, and you should be able to spot all the pits, but be cautious anyway.

"All right, each group move out, get in position, and when you hear me fire, you know the plan. Remember, the objective is to rescue the hostages, nothing else. Once the hostages are rescued we go to war, but not until then. Do not stray from the mission objective. Let's go!"

Adrian named each group after a letter of the alphabet in the time-honored military way. Alpha team was led by Jeff, and Adrian was with his group. Bravo team was led by Charles. Charlie team was led by Kyle and Delta team was led by George. Succession of command on the battlefield happened quite literally at the speed of a bullet. Naming a group after its leader was too confusing when a commander was killed. Therefore they were given names derived from the alphabet. In time, each group would come to believe that theirs was the best group of all. It was the way men were built, and the way armies improved. In fact, he could tell these men were already beginning, on their very first day, to follow the same tradition. "Good," he thought. "Very good."

The camp was a collection of buildings by a road with a stream bisecting part of it. It consisted of ten bunkhouse cabins, a main cabin, and a picnic pavilion. A small river ran through the camp, from West to East. The main cabin and the pavilion were on the North side of the river. The bunkhouse cabins were on the South side. They were joined by a pedestrian bridge located mid-way between the main cabin and the pavilion. The all-weather road came into the camp from the East. It went past the cabins and on West a half-mile to the mine head. It ran almost due east to the village, eleven miles away. It had been the truck route during the mine's operating days. The outhouses were located in the south-east quadrant of the camp, well away from everything else.

Bravo group circled the camp around the south side, staying back in the woods out of sight and achieving a position on the wood line to the west of the bunkhouse cabins. Two of Bravo group's best shots had dropped off at intervals, placing themselves on the edge of the woods at the nine o'clock and ten o'clock positions. The other four men in Bravo group waited at the eleven o'clock position. The two dropped off men were the best shots in the group and would act as snipers.

Charlie group also took position along the South perimeter, but at the five o'clock position. Their two best shots advanced along the perimeter to the seven and eight o'clock positions. Bravo and Charlie groups had the Southern arc of the mining camp well covered. They had a good view of the six bunkhouses. They could see portions of the main cabin, the bridge, and the pavilion between the cabins.

Delta took position east of the camp at the all-weather road, splitting up on either side of it, at the six o'clock position. They too were at the wood line where they could see the camp. Their view was an end-on view of the easternmost bunkhouse cabin, the pavilion, and up the road. They couldn't see much else.

Alpha took position Due North of the camp, at the point in the wood line closest to the pavilion; they were at the three o'clock. Their view was of the pavilion, the bridge, the main cabin, and the road. They could see portions of the bunkhouses between the pavilion and the main cabin. The perimeter of the camp from three o'clock to eleven o'clock was empty. Adrian did not need any men along that portion for this operation.

Adrian waited until he was sure each group had ample time to get into position. Wolfgang had taken to putting sentries on the roofs of some of the cabins, where they had a better view of the woods. Adrian aimed at the sentry closest to him, squeezed the trigger and watched the man flop backward as the bullet took him in the chest. Immediately he heard gunfire as the other men took their shots at sentries and the men walking about the camp.

Adrian's group fired no more shots. His shot was the signal for the other groups to attack. They were positioned to draw Wolfgang's men's attention away from the prisoners.

Bravo group advanced and fired, advanced and fired, as instructed, their two snipers remaining in position to provide covering fire and because their angle was best. Charlie group did exactly the same. Each groups mission was to advance to the halfway point of the open area, draw fire, then rapidly retreat to the woods as though in retreat. They were to force the enemy to engage with them and then hold their attention. He had instructed them to hold their ground at the wood line where there was plenty of cover, while Adrian's Alpha group ran across the open area to the pavilion, released the prisoners, and moved them down the road towards the village.

Adrian's group waited a few tense moments until he could tell by the sound of gunfire that Wolfgang's men were engaged and returning fire on the south side, then he and his five men stormed across the open area as fast as possible. There were two guards with the prisoners who had foolishly turned their backs to the North, thinking all the action was to the South. They heard the sound of running feet behind them too late...too late to do anything except die on the spot as Adrian and Jeff tackled them to the ground and stabbed them to death. While they were killing the two sentries, the Lieutenant and the other three men were hustling the villagers out of the pavilion and down the road, heading south as fast as they could make them go. So far the plan was working.

As the villagers were hustled past Delta, two men of Alpha stayed with them; they would stay with them all the way to the village, then return to the pre-determined rendezvous point to rejoin the battle. These were men that knew the area the best, frequent hunters. They would become scouts and were the best suited for the individual activities they were tasked with.

Adrian and Alpha's three remaining men joined Delta. They fired three rapid volleys of three shots each, the signal for Bravo and Charlie to retreat into the woods and disappear, then circle around to join up with Alpha and Delta along the road. They then moved east down the road a half-mile to a creek bed that gave them good cover. It was Adrian's guess that Wolfgang would launch an immediate attack on the only target he knew—the village. As he listened, he heard the sound of gunfire diminish rapidly. Bravo and Charlie had stopped firing and were circling the camp back to the road. The remaining sporadic and dwindling gun fire would be from Wolfgang's men firing at shadows.

Adrian was aware that Wolfgang's smartest move would be to regroup, fort up, and send out scouts to get information on who was out there and what they were up to. He was also aware that Wolfgang might be goaded into attacking the village after losing the prisoners. He hoped so. It would be a classic error if he did. Wolfgang still outnumbered Adrian's men, but a running battle in forest isn't the same thing as a battle on open ground. Terrain and cover could be used to one side's advantage, giving leverage to the force that had discipline and a fallback plan and rendezvous points. Adrian's Army had all those things. He knew the terrain intimately, how to use it, and when to withdraw. On top of that, he and his men had prearranged where to go if and when they did withdraw. It was an extension of his one-man war—deny the enemy a target.

Guerilla strategy and tactics were well assimilated in Adrian's mind from years of training followed by actual use. He knew how to effectively use a smaller force against a larger force. Adrian waited stoically for his two outbound groups to come in. It was a question now of what Wolfgang would do. Would he regroup? Would he come marching down the road? Or would he doing something unexpected? The best way to find out was to take a look. He called Jeff over. "You know the drill. Wait here for Bravo and Charlie groups. I'm going to do a little scouting and will be back before dark. Post sentries and tell them to keep an eye out for me; I don't want to be shot by my own men." Adrian selected one of the younger men to come along with him.

Without waiting for a reply he walked into the woods and disappeared. He strode swiftly back towards the mining camp, slowing as he approached the wood line. He crossed over the trail the dead roving patrol had used and belly-crawled the last few feet. He had no doubt that every available eye was scouring the wood's edges, searching for any sign of movement. When his eyes adjusted, he saw that not only had they accomplished their mission, but they had killed at least three of Wolfgang's men. He pointed them out to the man that had followed him. He could see the bodies lined up on the ground near the bridge. He saw Wolfgang marching up and down in front of his men, who were gathered in a loose formation. Wolfgang was gesturing wildly and looked as angry as Adrian had ever seen him, and Adrian had made him plenty angry on several occasions.

"Son, I believe they are about to attempt a punitive strike against the village," Adrian said, "which means they will be coming down the road. I am going back to set up the men. You keep watching, and if they go anywhere but down the road you come hauling ass back to me and tell me where they went. Don't forget to count how many of them there are. If they break up into groups, I need to know how many, what size, and where they're headed. If they head down the road as I suspect. you get back here and tell me as fast as you can. You'll have to run a wide circle around them through the woods, so run swiftly, but be safe. No shooting from you. I don't want them to know you've seen them. If they know you've seen them they'll do something different and that will cost us lives. Got all that?"

The young man nodded his head firmly.

Adrian quickly slipped back. He felt sure now that Wolfgang was coming down the road, in force—and in just a few minutes. "Ready or not, here they come!" he thought, as he sprinted through the woods back to his men.

CHAPTER 22

ADRIAND RETURNED TO THE CREEK bed and spread the word that Wolfgang's men would be coming down the road in a few minutes. "Listen up, I won't have time to repeat anything. No one fires until I do. Once I fire you open up with one immediate volley, choosing targets as best you can. Be warned that I won't open up until they are almost on top of us. It'll make you nervous, but hold your water and hold your fire until I shoot. Then fire one shot as soon as you can pick a target. After that, take your time. I want you to carefully sight in on a man, and slowly squeeze the trigger. Aim a little bit low or adrenaline will get your body all jacked up and make you jerk the trigger and miss.

"Better to shoot a little low and miss; your bullet might ricochet into your target or spray him with rocks. The main thing is, don't waste time by missing. It may seem unnatural to slow down and take your time when they are firing as fast as they can and bullets are flying all around you. Let them be the ones to shoot too fast and aim poorly. Don't you be an amateur like them. The old seasoned soldiers shoot just like they were on the rifle range. They take their time, they breathe out half a breath and hold it, then relax their muscles. Then they aim at a small and specific target, make sure they have a good sight alignment with both sights, and squeeze the trigger. And by God, they hit something. I want you men to slow down, and do the same thing. Remember the word 'brass.' It stands for breathe, relax, aim, sight, and squeeze. Do it in sequence as you spell out the word in your head. Be damn certain you are aiming at a button on a shirt, or an eyeball, or something else small. Don't just aim at the whole man.

"Do all these things and you will send them running back to their camp like whipped dogs. Don't do these things and they will send you running to your women like whipped dogs. Is that clear? Good. I'll be walking up and down the line behind you, giving advice, helping where I can. I'll be coaching and watching. If I see anyone hurrying a shot or getting panicky, I'll pull you out of the line and make you sit the fight out. One panicky man can start others to act the same way. Anyone pulled out for panicking has to wait ten minutes before he can get back in. Ten minutes is a hell of a long time in a firefight, and believe me, you'll wish to hell you hadn't panicked, especially when everyone else stayed calm.

"Take up your positions and be ready. No shooting until I shoot. Quiet now, and don't do anything to give our position away. If they're smart they'll send scouts ahead of them, looking for an ambush. If they do I'll let the scouts go on past. You, you and you," Arian said, pointing to three men. "If scouts go past, your job is to follow them and kill them before they can come back up behind us—but you don't leave until I shoot. Then you go and kill them. OK, get ready, they should be along shortly."

The young man detailed to stay behind and watch the camp came out of the woods, out of breath and excited. He came up to Adrian and saluted. Adrian, amused, saluted back. "Sir, they are all coming down the road. The same group we watched. I waited a couple of minutes to be sure no one else was leaving after them—none did."

"Good job, soldier, and good thinking on waiting the extra time. They might have tried to pull a fast one and you would have caught them. Well done!" Adrian watched as the young man's stature stiffened with pride, as though he had gained ten years' confidence from that small bit of public praise. "Praise in public and chew out in private," Adrian thought. "It's always been top advice."

Five long and tense minutes later Adrian spotted Wolfgang's men coming down the road. There were no scouts. The men were in two single-file lines on either side of the road. One shot and the men would quickly disappear into the brush beside the road; it was imperative to wait until they were as close as possible. Adrian had hoped that Wolfgang would be in front of his men and easy to pick off, but he was in the rear of the left-hand column. "Cowardly bastard," Adrian thought. "But a strong sense of self-preservation typical of a psychopath."

Glancing at his men to his left he could see that they were as ready as they were nervous, but holding position. Each man was following a target. Looking to his right he could see the same. These men were as green as anyone could be. This was their first day in combat, and with no training at all, just advice. But they were fighting for their homes and families. Their mothers and wives and daughters and friends were behind them, depending on them to keep them safe. These men wouldn't run. If he could keep them calm and steady they would be the deadliest fighting men on the field today. Nothing firms a man's resolution like fighting for his home.

Wolfgang's men, on the other hand, probably had little idea why they were fighting. They had been harassed and picked off for months. They were angry and ready for revenge, but their quality was far from those of Adrian's men. They wouldn't even be fighting if they didn't know they had an advantage in number. They should have learned from Adrian that numbers weren't everything, but apparently they needed another lesson. Adrian carefully took aim at the man furthest back that he could see and waited. He waited until the man in front was thirty yards away. Then twenty, then ten. He waited until the man in front caught sight of Adrian's men. He waited as that man stopped and was bumped by the man behind him. He waited until that man figured out what was happening and opened his mouth to shout the alarm. Then Adrian fired.

His men had been ready to pull triggers for ages before Adrian fired. When he did, they all jerked the trigger in reflex. Men were falling, jumping for the woods, taking cover behind men in front of them while they tried to figure out what to do. Men were screaming and bleeding. Men were fumbling for their rifles and two or three men tried to return fire. All in the space of a second. The first volley ripped bullets through chests and heads and legs.

Adrian carefully aimed and squeezed off two more shots, hitting his targets each time. Now it was time for Adrian to see to his men. He couldn't carry this battle on his own, though he could do one hell of a lot of damage. What he could do best now was show these men how to vanquish their enemy. He moved along the line from man to man, watching each man as he chose a target and fired. Adrian gave pats on the back and words of encouragement. He had no intention of trying to embarrass or correct any of these men at this moment, unless one of them was over the edge with panic. Even then, a few encouraging words, a reminder on the meaning of the acronym brass, and a pat on the back would do more good than anything else at a moment like that.

His men were pouring a slow and lethal fire into Wolfgang's men. They were doing as told, taking their time, and shooting with deadly efficiency. Wolfgang's men had moved into the forest edge on both sides of the road. They were panicked, and their bullets were mostly flying high, thudding into trees and breaking off limbs over the heads of Adrian's men. Wolfgang was taking a beating. Adrian had held one group back as a quick strike team in the event that Wolfgang tried a flanking movement. It would have been a good move on his part, but unless his men were trained in combat maneuvers, it would have been difficult to carry off. There was also the element of time. Darkness would be descending soon. Wolfgang didn't have a lot of time to experiment, so Adrian made the choice to move the strike force to the front line.

Adrian knew that Wolfgang had two other options: a full frontal assault or retreat back to the cabins. A full frontal assault would be disastrous against the withering fire Adrian's men were putting into their opponents, and he doubted that Wolfgang could persuade his men to even try it. Withdrawal was probably only moments away. Adrian moved up and down the line, warning his men to stay in position no matter what came next. Under no circumstances was any man to try and follow a retreat. He didn't want to lose his men due to stupidity. They had won two major encounters today without a single injury so far. They had put a frightful hurting on the enemy. Being too greedy wasn't going to win this war—intelligence was.

Adrian had been constantly on the watch for a shot at Wolfgang, but the man had stayed completely out of sight. As he watched, Wolfgang's men began a slow disengagement. The men in front were pulling back from tree to tree while the men in back gave covering fire. Adrian's men were still shooting effectively. Once the battle had stabilized they had gotten into a very good rhythm of fire. They couldn't have done better. Within twenty minutes from the first shot, the firing had trickled to a stop. Adrian checked his men—two minor injuries. He sent scouts out to check the camp perimeter and report back. Adrian walked carefully through the woods where Wolfgang's men had taken cover. They hadn't taken their dead with them, and had left two critically wounded, dying in the dirt. Pulling out his pistol he shot them in the head. He had no way to take care of prisoners. He counted the bodies. Thirteen dead, no telling how many wounded. "Excellent. Just beautifully excellent. These are some fighting sons-of-bitches."

He went back to his men. "Gather round, men. I shot two wounded men. We can't take prisoners, we can't keep prisoners, we can't guard prisoners, we can't feed prisoners, and we can't turn enemies loose to ambush us later. There will be no prisoners. This is a war to the complete death of every single enemy. Does anyone want to talk about it? If you know of a way to do this better, I am listening."

There were several seconds of silence as the men looked at each other or Adrian or down at their feet. It was not something they had contemplated, and they didn't like it. But it was reality.

"I don't like it either, but remember, you didn't ask these assholes to attack your village or kill and eat people. They get what they deserve—death. Remember that they won't treat you any differently, except they may let you lie there and die slowly, then roast you for dinner.

We'll be moving all night. You men have performed so much better than I could have dreamed of... there are no words to tell you how proud I am of you. I would be happy to lead you men into hell and take on the devil himself. What you have done in one day is impossible, yet I watched you do it. Now it's time to dig deep and find the resolve to keep at it. Tomorrow has more bad things in store for Wolfgang. I think I know what his next move will be, but I'm not sure of the exact direction it will come from."

CHAPTER 23

"THINK LIKE HE DOES. FIGURE out what he will have to do next. He knows only one way to survive—taking from others. He doesn't have the skills to be self-sufficient. He has the skills to brutalize and steal. He has always been a wolf among sheep. Now he is faced with a simple problem—how to neutralize a superior force. And we, men, are that force.

"My thought is that he will try to work his way behind us and get into the village, take the village hostage, and demand our surrender. He kills three birds with one stone. He secures food, neutralizes our fighting ability, and creates a secure base. His old base is no longer tenable.

"Here's what we're going to do. We'll post lookouts near his camp to watch for his departure, which I think will come at about three this morning because he will want to sneak past us in the dark and arrive at dawn. We will post scouts across the areas that he is most likely to travel. Scouts will have a central return point to report to. First sign of movement, and once they know his men's direction, and the scout rushes back to us so we can move into ambush position. We'll need scouts to continue to watch them in case they change direction, so scouts will be in pairs—one to report and one to continue to track their direction.

This means we'll largely be scattered out in the forest without communication. The camp scouts will stay in position until Wolfgang has moved out. The scouts in the forest will return after daybreak to the rendezvous point. Keep your ears open for gunfire. If you hear gunfire, move towards it immediately, come around from the south side, our side, and join in the fight. Night fighting is extremely difficult; I know you're thinking about that. Just remember, it is as hard on them as it is on you, so it equalizes out and you remain the superior force."

Adrian then assigned men to scout duty and told them where to position themselves. Over half the men were involved in the scouting, leaving a small strike force to respond to the eventual incoming information. He was aware that this small group would have to hold all of Wolfgang's men at bay until the rest of the men returned to the battle. It worried him, but the camp was not a good target to attack. Wolfgang would hole up in the cabins and any attempt to attack across open ground would incur too many casualties. Setting the cabins on fire would expose the men to counterattack, because Wolfgang would be waiting for some such tactic.

The best bet would be to locate them on the move in the forest, get ahead of them in a good spot, and repeat the drubbing they had already given them once. This time, their forces would be reduced to the point that pursuing them through the woods, although extremely dangerous, would be necessary. Otherwise the survivors would be able to regroup yet again and find another opportunity to attack the village. They would inevitably be drawn back by the promise of food, the only large supply they knew of. There were three tribes in the area they could attack, each one an opportunity for food, and probably they would attack them before taking on the village. Once scattered out they would be hard to locate and destroy.

After the scouts had departed, Adrian gathered the remaining men. "Try to rest. If you can sleep, do so. I don't think we'll be here more than a few hours before we are hustling to a new location, so while we are waiting, rest. Soldiers learn quickly to eat and sleep when they can."

As the men rested, Adrian sat and waited. Waiting made him edgy. He was restless, willing the action to come but hoping it could be held until daylight when they would be able to see. Night fighting with untrained men and no communication was a bad proposition, perhaps unavoidable, but not something these men were really ready or equipped for. The fairly strong moonlight would help, but perhaps not enough.

His thoughts drifted to Alice. He had felt her presence with him—nothing supernatural but still real to him—he had felt her until the moment he almost died himself. Her presence had been strongest as he was dying. But since awakening in a rage he hadn't felt her, not until he saw the hostages at the camp. As soon as he saw the hostages, the feeling of her had come roaring back. He was aware that he could now think of her without shutting down. The pain was still there, but buried deeper and a tiny bit muted. That ache would never go away, but he could tell that it would decrease until he could live with it. It was the first time he had begun to believe that paint might level off; Roman had been right again.

Adrian was also aware that he had rediscovered a

talent for leading men into battle, training them, and teaching them how to fight. The pride he felt in these men was a strong emotion, one of deep satisfaction. He was beginning to realize that perhaps his mission in life was to help people defend themselves. Organizing and training and leading them as conditions warranted. His thoughts cast back to the Palo Duro Canyon and the group he had found there. In a very short time he had led them from despair and starvation to a functioning tribe with hope and direction and a future. He had felt pride in the accomplishment at the time, but it had been overwhelmed by bitter sorrow.

He also recognized that he had left Fort Brazos with a death wish. It wasn't that he had wanted to explore, but that he had gone seeking death, the only release from the pain he could think of. It explained his immediate attack on the grizzly bear with only a flint-tipped spear. It explained his continued risk of the guerrilla warfare he employed against Wolfgang. As long as it was just him and Wolfgang, that could have gone on for a long time. Seeing the hostages had changed that. Seeing them had snapped him back to himself. He had, for the briefest of moments, resented the hostages for taking away his game. But realization that it wasn't their fault, and that his game had been one of selfish meanness, had swiftly overcome it. Adrian came to the full realization that his actions against Wolfgang and his men had been over the border of sanity. He was almost repulsed by his own actions against these men; almost but not quite. They had deserved that treatment and worse. Seeing now what he was capable of descending to shook him up badly.

His thoughts returned to the upcoming battle. He was confident that they could win, destroy the enemy, and bring an end to the threat. His concern was for his men. Leading them into the battle without losing any of them was his goal. These men had shown extraordinary courage, and would be forever changed by this day. They were good men, the kind this world needed now in the worst kind of way. When this was over, he might head back home, secure in the knowledge that these men would protect their village against all enemies in the future. They would have discipline and order and, most importantly, experience. They had received an overnight instruction in how to fight effectively. He had two missions: destroy Wolfgang with these men while trying to keep them safe from harm. It was a tall order.

One of the camp scouts returned at four in the morning. "They snuck out an hour ago, took a course to the Southwest. They started off following the draw that leads down the mountain. I followed a little ways to make sure."

Another scout came in, one that had been posted to the Southwest. "They're coming, slowly, but coming down the draw."

"Take two men and gather the rest of the scouts back in," Adrian ordered the scouts. "Tell them to meet us on the south side of the meadow with the big rock in the middle. I think they'll be coming that way. Quickly, we don't have much time. The rest of you, follow me. Tell the scouts to use the password."

Adrian led the men to the meadow and put them in position. "Do not fire until I do. Fire as quickly as you can get on a target. We want to kill as many as we can before they run away, which I believe they will. I won't shoot until the very last possible second."

They had been in position for a nerve wracking forty

minutes before they spotted movement. The men were alert and nervous, but more confident than before. The moon was at its apex and the light was as good as it was going to get that night. Adrian was grateful for no cloud cover. This mission would have been impossible in complete darkness. He checked each man once more, giving words of individual encouragement and reminders to fire as rapidly as accuracy allowed.

Adrian watched as the remaining mobile men of Wolfgang's group finally entered the moonlit meadow. A tactical mistake made by rank amateurs. They had been in the dark forest for so long that he knew they felt relief to be out where they could see again. They had no idea that they had just walked into their own death trap. Instead they thought they had gone around the threat. Adrian waited while they came across the meadow towards him. They were strung out, moving slowly and talking quietly now and then. They had nearly zero battle discipline. The smart move would have been to avoid the meadow and stay in the forest, maneuvering around its edge. These men were not soldiers, they were thugs that had banded together out of convenience. They were not a unit, they were individuals working together in a rough fashion. Their leader was a brutish psychopath and not very smart. Adrian's main fear now was that they would scatter before being killed, making them difficult to locate and finish off.

He waited and watched as they came closer. He waited until they all passed the big rock and were almost on top of him, then he fired at the man farthest back, hoping it was Wolfgang. The meadow's south edge erupted in gunfire. Several of the scouts were still out, but Adrian knew they would be close by. They would hear the gunfire and come up behind them. He had alerted his men to this fact, to be extremely careful of shooting at anyone behind the opposing side. "Even if a few get behind us," he had warned, "they won't be much of a threat. Better to let them go and find them later than to shoot one of our own. Not an ideal situation, but it's the best we can do right now."

The men fired steadily, knocking down the men in the meadow quickly. Two made it back into the forest and disappeared. The shooting stopped. It had only lasted a minute. His men were deadly fighters. He called them together, took a head count, and checked for injuries. One more gunshot wound, serious but not life threatening. It was the only damage. Adrian was extraordinarily relieved. All of the scouts were back; the full contingent was in place.

"All right ,men, good job. Damn good job. Return to the village, post guards around the perimeter. This war is over. There are two men that got away and I am willing to bet Wolfgang was one of them. I'm going after him. I need one volunteer to go with me, to help watch my back." Every man quickly raised his hand, including the two wounded soldiers.

"That's the spirit. That's what I love about you, men. You've got guts like I've never seen!" Every chest swelled with pride. General Bear, as they had taken to calling him privately, was proud of them. They admired everything about him, would lay their lives down for him, and he was telling them he loved them. Their spirits lifted higher than they had ever experienced, victorious in battle twice in twenty-four hours, adrenaline still surging. They had become warriors with the best war leader ever, and they loved him in the way men love each other in times of war.

Adrian picked one man, the one that scouted the camp and returned first. He had shown initiative twice and was fast on his feet, so he had the best chance of keeping up with Adrian. "Come on, we have to move fast. I've a hunch as to where they will be going and if I'm right we can cut them off. You men finish off any survivors, collect any useful guns and ammo, and return to the village. Tomorrow take half the men and go to their camp and finish of the wounded ones. It's a hard duty to kill those men, but it's what has to be done. Make sure you choose men who have the ability to live with it the rest of their lives. We'll be back in a few days." Adrian quickly checked the bodies, looking for Wolfgang, and wasn't surprised to find him missing. With that, they disappeared into the dark forest.

CHAPTER 24

THEY TRAVELLED THROUGH THE DARK forest at a fast walk, heading at an angle off from the meadow. Greg asked, "Where do you think they're going?" "Remember that small tribe about ten miles northwest of the camp? I'm sure Wolfgang knows of it. It's as far from the village as he can get right now and still be in territory he knows. My hunch is he will head there, take over the tribe by killing the leader, and take their food. He'll rest there for a couple of days while deciding what to do next. We want to get there ahead of him."

As the sun came up they traveled faster, moving at double-time. They didn't stop to rest. They moved relentlessly forward across the rough terrain. Wolfgang had a head start, but Adrian thought he could travel faster. Wolfgang would stop to rest occasionally; he wouldn't know that he needed to hurry. Adrian wouldn't stop and knew where he was going. He intended to get ahead of them, find a likely ambush spot, and finish them off once and for all. It wasn't rocket science, but it was hard work, and required determination. Assuming Wolfgang did as Adrian thought he would, the plan would work.

They had been at it for several hours and the sun had started to peak over the mountain tops. As they started across a large creek, a Grizzly bear with two cubs loomed up in front of them. The bear roared and started to attack in defense of her cubs. Adrian shouted to Greg,"Don't shoot! Don't run!" He then hollered as loud as he could right at the bear, letting out a hair-raising Texas rebel yell. The bear stopped in confusion. She was surprised that the man didn't run and was confused by his ear-splitting yell. She stood looking at Adrian, swaying her head back from side to side, trying to get a better look. Then she flared her nostrils and sucked in air to get a good smell of him.

When she breathed in his scent, her demeanor changed entirely. She went from ferocious mother defending her cubs to practically uninterested. She approached without antagonism or fear. As she got closer, Adrian stood his ground. He couldn't outrun her, but a small voice in the back of his mind told him not to shoot her. He stood as she came closer. Greg, a few yards behind Adrian, watched, rifle cocked and aimed, dying to shoot. But Adrian had told him not to and he would not disobey, no matter what.

The bear came close to Adrian and took another small sniff. The she took a large whiff of his scent. She came closer and looked at him closely. Adrian stood his ground, suddenly smiling. This was the sow he had shared the den with after his head wound. She had recognized his scent, a scent she had inhaled in close proximity for a week, although mostly covered by the bear scent on him. She'd had her cubs already. They came up and milled around her feet. The bear turned toward Greg and growled low but loud, a clear warning, then turned around and left with the cubs running ahead of her, disappearing into the forest as if they had never been.

A long moment passed, Adrian turned to Greg and said, "That's the bear I slept with. She recognized my odor. Pretty as a picture isn't she?"

Greg looked at Adrian with a mixture of confusion, fading fear and shock. "Slept with her? A grizzly bear?"

"Sure. I'd been grazed across the skull with a bullet, had a concussion, and Wolfgang was chasing me. Damn near caught me too, but I found a hole under a tree and crawled inside and passed out. I was out for about a week I think, sleeping right up against that old girl. But enough of fond memories, let's get moving." Little did Adrian know his statement and explanation would grow into another enormous myth that would explode like wildfire across the ham radio internet and then the entire country. A story that would precede him wherever he went for the rest of his life. A story he would never be allowed to explain in a rational way. Adrian's stories would go viral on the ham radio, the new internet.

Two hours before dark, they came to the edge of the tribe's area. There were plenty of signs that the people of the tribe were in close proximity. Adrian said, "I don't want to alert the tribe; it would take too long to explain and they can't help us anyway. We'll scout around and try to figure out the best place to set up." It took him just over an hour to find a good observation spot that gave a wide view of the direction that Wolfgang should be coming from. They had climbed a stony ridge that looked down over a vast sweeping area. From there, they could see several miles and had a good chance of spotting Wolfgang.

"We'll watch until dark, then make a cold camp. No fire for us tonight. We'll look for their campfire after dark.

If we're lucky, Wolfgang will make a fire for the night and then he's dead before daybreak." They sat and watched, memorizing the lay of the land in the fading light. Adrian pointed out a particular defile that crossed much of the area. "That's most likely the way he'll come. It's a natural pathway."

They looked for fire after dark, but saw none. "We'll take turns sleeping; I'll take first watch and wake you when it's your turn." Adrian sat, wide awake, and went over and over his reasoning. He couldn't find a flaw in his logic, but knew that logic could only take him so far. The rest was up to intuition and fate. He thought about the bear and realized that the reason he couldn't eat bear meat now was because some sort of bond had formed between him and the mother grizzly while they were together in the den. The thought of killing a bear now turned his stomach, and he knew he would never kill another one.

When Greg relieved him from his watch, he lay down and was asleep in seconds. He dreamed of Alice and felt her approval of his actions since the hostages were taken, but felt no approval of his war before that. No disapproval either. His mind was projecting into his dreams what she would have thought about it all. She would not have thought of his war as something he should have devoted so much passion to. But she might have understood it as a distraction from grief. He was awakened before dawn by Greg, as instructed.

They set up watch on the ridge again, straining to see any movement in the early light as the sun came up. "For observation, two sets of eyes are much better than one," Adrian told Greg. "Watch for movement of any kind." They spotted elk and deer grazing. At one point

Adrian thought he spotted a bear, but wasn't sure. It was backbreaking work to stare that long and hard, trying to force a sighting. "This can get boring," Adrian warned. "It's mentally fatiguing to stay at it with concentration, but it has to be done. Don't let your mind wander. Close your eyes now and then for thirty seconds to rest them. But not too often and let me know when you do, I'll do the same."

Unexpectedly, a thick fog began rolling into the valley. Adrian watched and knew that the fog changed everything. "Greg, change of plans. This fog is going to get really thick in a few minutes; it's moving in fast. You go on to the tribe and let them know what I'm doing. I doubt that they will be moving out of their camp in this, but to be extra sure to tell them to wait there for me. The way I'm going to have to do this, I won't be able to see faces very well and I don't want to make a mistake. Hurry, before it gets here and you get lost."

"What are you going to do?"

"No time now to explain, I'll tell you all about it later. Get going. Hurry! Wait! Give me your cooking pot and bedroll—quickly now." Greg looked at him with curiosity, but complied and left.

Adrian took one long, last hard look at the valley, reinforcing key features in his memory that he would recognize in the fog when he got close enough to see them, and placed them in his mind in relation to the other key features. He moved swiftly to get into the spot he had chosen as the most likely place that Wolfgang would walk through, or near, to get to the tribe camp. He scrambled down the ridge, knocking rocks and dirt loose as he went. He didn't have time for finesse.

When he reached his target area he swiftly gathered

dry wood. He gathered enough to make a fire that would last for several hours. He broke some of the wood up, made a separate pile, and quickly lit it on fire. As soon as the fire was burning he placed the cooking pot next to the fire. Unrolling the bedroll, he made a bed near the fire on the side opposite from where Wolfgang would approach. Still moving hurriedly he stripped to his shorts and laid his clothes on the bedroll.

Adrian gathered dry grass from around him until he had enough. He used it to stuff his clothes, making a dummy of himself sleeping. It wasn't great, but in the fog and behind the fire he thought it might do the trick. He placed a rock about the size of his head at the top of the stuffed shirt, threw the edge of the bedroll on it, and then surveyed the scene. It wouldn't fool anyone on a clear day, but in the fog it might. He then took of his boots and placed them near the fire as the final touch.

Clad only in his boxer shorts, he took his rifle and knife and found a good hiding spot behind a thick bush just a scant fifteen feet away. Using cordage he tied the knife scabbard to his thigh. Now it was time to wait. If his plan worked, the smell of smoke and the glow of the campfire would catch Wolfgang's attention. He was hoping against the odds that Wolfgang would be hungry enough to keep moving in the fog. There was absolutely no he could find Wolfgang in the fog, but he might draw Wolfgang to him if he had guessed correctly where Wolfgang would be coming from. The fog had settled in and visibility was down to only a few feet. He hoped it didn't lift at the wrong time. If it did, not only would his plan fail, but he might find himself badly exposed to rifle fire.

Adrian was a patient hunter. It was hard to tell what time it was with no visible sun, but his internal clock told him that at least an hour had gone by. Twice he had quietly moved to put more wood on the fire. It was important that the flames were bright. Each time he refreshed the fire he was taking a chance that Wolfgang would come up on him at that moment. The damp woods and the fog made moving quietly easy for anyone, and when he came, Wolfgang would be arriving in stealth mode. He would be looking for a chance for easy food. It was his style and Adrian was counting on it.

Another hour passed. Adrian was cold and cramped, but held his position. He was on full alert, ears and eyes straining as hard as possible for any sign that Wolfgang was near. The fire was low again.

Adrian eased over to the fire and a stinging sensation struck his right arm, above the elbow, instantly accompanied by the sound of a rifle shot. Adrian instinctively and immediately rolled away from the fire into the fog. leaving his rifle behind. He pulled out his bowie knife, crouched, and waited for a second, then he quietly moved off to the right several paces. Another shot rang out. Adrian wasn't hit, and he couldn't tell where the rifle had been aimed. He guessed that Wolfgang had fired into the area where Adrian had been only a moment ago. Adrian threw himself on the ground, making the sound of a body landing, let out a low groan, then quietly jumped to his feet and moved off again a couple of yards. He wanted Wolfgang to believe he had been hit again.

Adrian checked his arm. It was a through and through shot, hitting muscle but not bone. He was bleeding badly, but not spurting from an artery. Blood loss would weaken him soon, and this was no time for weakness. He was on the clock now. He had to make this happen, and soon, or he would grow too weak to be effective. Adrian lay down flat and listened. He heard a slight crunching sound of boots on soil.

Slowly the outlines of two men came into view. They stayed close enough together to see each other, but no closer. They were only five yards away from Adrian, and they were five yards apart, the three of them making a triangle. They were looking in the wrong direction, but as soon as either one shifted his eyes to the right Adrian would be visible. His knife against two armed killers. Adrian liked the odds.

Slowly, Adrian gathered himself into a crouching position. His naked skin was nearly snow white from the long winter, and he blended in with the fog better than they did in their dark clothing. Adrian achingly reached a fully loaded, crouched position and then silently launched himself at the nearest of the two men. He reached the man before he could react. Adrian hit him with a full body tackle at the same moment that he plunged his knife into the man's throat, the point of his blade exiting the back of his neck.

Adrian kept rolling forward as he pulled the knife free, tumbling away from the thrashing body. The other man shot at him in a reflexive action, missing Adrian by a fraction of an inch spraying him with stinging gravel. Adrian stopped his forward motion, sprang sideways, rolled, and came up on his feet, instantly launching himself at the other man. This maneuver had kept him from being able to line his rifle up on Adrian, so the man used it as a club instead, swinging at Adrian with a brutal butt stroke. Adrian used his injured right arm as a shield. It was all it was good for at the moment, absorbing the punishing blow on top of the gunshot wound. Searing paint jolted through Adrian's body like lightning.

Adrian pressed on with his attack and slashed out with a backhand cut that deeply cut the man, who quickly fled, disappearing into the fog. Adrian had lost sight of him, but knew he was badly cut and would leave a blood trail. He had cut him deeply but he wasn't sure where, wasn't sure it was a killing cut. He now had to trail the main in the thick fog. He set out slowly, looking for a blood trail and following it. This was dangerous; he could walk up on him at any moment and be shot. The wounded man would be on the alert and Adrian was wounded as well. The odds weren't good but he wouldn't back off and wait; he was too close to give up. As Adrian followed the blood trail he occasionally stopped to listen intently. He was hoping that his quarry would make some small sound and give away his position.

The blood trail was diminishing. Whatever wound it was, it wasn't arterial and the blood loss was slowing. There wasn't enough blood to indicate a significant wound. Adrian crept on, hoping that the blood trail wouldn't end. It was difficult to find in the fog, trailing off and then occasionally reappearing. Adrian kept following, knowing he was exposed, and had only a knife and his wits against a rifle. His quarry, whether Wolfgang or not had the advantage. All he had to do was sit still and wait for Adrian to appear, then shoot.

He kept going, and had covered perhaps an eighth of a mile when the blood trail gave out completely. He stood there, unsure what to do next—perhaps go back to camp and get his rifle and wait for the fog to lift. Then he heard a small sound in front of him. In the fog it was hard to tell where or what or how far away. Adrian clenched his knife in his teeth and threw a rock to the right of where he thought the sound came from, re-gripping his knife before the rock could land. A rifle shot rang out directly in front of him. Adrian charged as fast as he could run and ran right into Wolfgang as he was working the bolt for a second shot. He hit Wolfgang with a full body tackle, swarming all over him and knocking the rifle loose from his grip, the two of them tumbling down together. Wolfgang was strong and foul smelling. Adrian plunged his knife deep into Wolfgang's chest and held his eyes with his own, watching the man's life ebb away. Adrian slowly got up, weak from blood loss, and followed the blood trail back to camp. He saw the glow of the fire with relief.

He sat down abruptly. The combination of the gunshot wound, the blood loss, the punishing butt stroke and the final fight, all underscored by rushing adrenalin, made him faint to nearly black out. He was nauseous and threw up bile. Adrian sat there for a few more minutes, gathered his strength and stood. He stumbled over to the fire and poured water from his canteen into the cook pot and set it on the fire to boil. Then he reclaimed his clothes from the dummy and dressed. He dragged the bedroll close to the fire and pulled it over him like a robe, absorbing the warmth of the nearby flames.

When the water boiled, Adrian cut off a piece of bedroll and using a clean portion of it dabbed it into the boiling water and began to clean his wound. It was an ugly hole going in and even uglier coming out. There was already a bruise forming from the gun's butt. He washed the wound as well as he could, then he boiled the cloth in the water for a minute and used it again as a bandage. The bleeding had slowed but hadn't stopped. The bandage was soon soaked. Adrian had to stop this bleeding or he would be in serious trouble.

He took the bandage off and put it in the water to boil again. Then he took a knife off the body nearby, and put the blade into the fire to heat. When it was red hot he picked it up and pressed the blade flat against the entry wound, until the raw meat was cauterized. The smell of his burning flesh and the searing pain nearly made him pass out. He vomited again. Again, he placed the knife blade into the fire and sat rocking back and forth, trying to stem the pain as he waited. The bleeding had nearly stopped on the entry side, but the backside was still bleeding freely. He had to stop it.

Adrian pulled the knife out when it was red hot again, and painfully twisting his arm around applied the knife blade to the exit wound. He held it there as long as he could—this was a bigger hole. He held it there until it cooled off. It took every ounce of will power he could muster to hold it against his flesh. The bleeding was almost stopped, but there was still non-cauterized flesh inside the hole. Once more Adrian placed the knife in the fire and waited. Using just the knife's tip he spot cauterized inside the wound until the bleeding stopped. Then he fainted.

Adrian came to a few minutes later, washed the wound one more time with the boiling hot bandage, then, when the bandage cooled enough, wrapped it around his arm. He desperately wanted to lie down, but the fog was lifting and he knew he had better get to the tribe's camp while he still had some strength left.

CHAPTER 25

THE SMELL OF SMOKE TOLD Adrian that he was near the tribe's camp, he began shouting "Hallo the camp!" It wouldn't be a good idea to appear to be sneaking in. He shouted three times before Greg and another man armed with a shotgun came running out to him.

The man lowered his shotgun and shouted, "All clear!" Four men, five women, and three children appeared from behind fallen trees and boulders at the edge of the forest. All of the adults were armed. The children hung back.

"Welcome, Adrian. I'm Martin. We've heard a lot about you. Glad to meet you. Come and sit down. You're injured—how bad is it? Allyson! Come take a look at Bear's arm."

Adrian was startled by the woman's name since it was so close to that of his wife. He was equally nonplussed by being called Bear. He knew that nicknames were spontaneously awarded and often stuck for life. He was probably stuck with this one. "What do you think about that, Alice?" he thought. "You would probably have loved it and given me hell about it." Adrian sat on a handcrafted bench, his tension releasing. He was weak and in considerable pain, but he was alive and was healthy. He would heal; Wolfgang was dead. That was what counted.

"Have you eaten?" Martin asked. "We have fresh elk. Jenna, would you be so kind as to cook this man some steak? He looks hungry."

Adrian's stomach, alerted to the possibility of incoming food, began growling loudly. He was suddenly ravenous. "Thank you, I am a bit hungry at that."

"Greg filled us in. Did you kill those two men? I'm guessing you did or they would be here instead."

"Just a little while ago." While he ate, Adrian told them the whole story, ending with the death of Wolfgang. The elk steak was delicious and refreshing. Martin asked about the sow grizzly. Adrian repeated the story to everyone's amazement.

Adrian rested for four days, letting the wound heal some and replacing the lost blood. He ate a lot of fresh steak and bone marrow, and quickly regained his strength.

As they were saying their goodbyes to start their journey back, Martin teased Adrian. "Man that story is going to really get around. I can hear it now: 'General Hunter is so tough he sleeps with grizzly bears and has cubs all over the mountains.'" Martin laughed aloud.

"That is some story!" Adrian smiled ruefully. It was all he could do. This was a cross he would have to "bear" the rest of his life, and he knew it.

"That's not quite how it happened, but I don't suppose there's much point in trying to straighten that out, is there?"

"Oh no, it's too good. Way too good as it is."

Adrian and Greg left the tribe on good terms with promises of future visits and trade. They camped for the night halfway to the village. As they sat by the fire, cooking more elk steaks, Adrian said, "You know Greg, I would just as soon that bear story died right here."

Greg said, "I don't think that's possible. Even if I promised never to tell the story, Martin will. With those scars showing on your neck and face, you're always going to be called "Bear," no escaping that. Martin will visit the village and tell the story and it will spread from there. Sorry about telling him, but I didn't know you wanted to keep your girlfriend a secret." Adrian threw a stick at Greg who laughingly dodged out of the way.

They arrived at the village the next evening. As they came in the entire village poured out to meet them. The villagers were as happy as any people Adrian had ever seen. They gave a hero's welcome. A banquet was quickly assembled and the old woman gave a speech.

"Ladies and Gentlemen, it is with great honor and gratitude that we present General Hunter with this symbol of our appreciation. Adrian, please step up here so that I can give you this medal." Adrian stood and walked to the front. The old woman, Francis, he had learned, opened a small decorated box and removed a gold lapel pin that had been handmade by an artisan in the village. It was solid 14K gold and the size of a silver dollar, with a pin on the back. It showed a grizzly bear with two cubs.

Adrian looked at the medal and laughed. "Thank you, but I have to be honest and tell you all that this is not my medal—this is your men's medal. Everything that happened after Wolfgang took hostages was because of their courage and bravery. Every one of them is a true hero. But, on their behalf I will accept this and wear it proudly." There was loud applause and cheering.

That night Adrian lay in a bed for the first time in

nearly a year. He couldn't sleep. His life had changed and he didn't know what he was going to do next. He tossed and turned and thought all night long, but came to no conclusions. He believed that his best use was to train and lead men into battle. He was not a peacetime person, and probably wouldn't be until he was in his grave.

In the morning, Francis sat next to him at breakfast. "I talked to your uncle Roman on the radio last night. I've talked to him several times over the past year. He would ask every now and then if we had seen you or heard anything about you. All I could do was to pass on the rumors we heard of your war, the same stories that have spread everywhere. I called him last night and told him you were back here safe and sound, and presumably sane. He was mighty glad to hear it and told me to tell you that he and Sarah love and miss you. He also asked if you would radio him when you woke up. He has something urgent to discuss."

Adrian jumped up, leaving his breakfast unfinished. "Where's the radio?"

"Adrian? Is that you son? My God, it's good to hear your voice. How are you? Sarah's right here too."

"Hey Aunt Sarah! I'm doing great. I'm with good friends right now and healthy as I can expect to be. How is everyone?"

After the small talk was over Adrian said, "Francis tells me you have some urgent business to discuss?"

"Son, we have trouble down here. Big trouble. You need to come home; we need your help in the worst kind of way. Will you come?"

"I'll come straight there. But what kind of trouble?"

"I hate to raise your curiosity like that and not lay it back down, but I don't want to talk about it on the radio.

Too many ears. How long do you think it'll take?

"I can make it in four or five weeks. I'll leave first thing tomorrow morning. I need to assemble some kit first."

"Great. Travel carefully, talk to no one on the way, especially as you get close in, but hurry every chance you get. I would rather no one knows you're coming. Time is of the essence now."

They said their goodbyes and Francis said, "Tell me what you need and I'll find it all today. Also, we have some horses; you can make much better time if you take one. "

"That's a deal, Francis. I can cut the time in half and it sounds like I need to. Thanks."

Adrian left on horseback, riding as rapidly as the creature could sustain. Whenever the horse would begin to tire, Adrian would dismount and walk the horse for half an hour, then Adrian would trot a half hour. Then with the horse rested from his weight he would ride again. After two days he came across a dead wolf lying outside her den entrance. A lone wolf pup was snuggled up to her, the pup just past the weaning stage. It was weak with hunger but refused to run from Adrian and snarled, standing over its mother's body. Adrian pounced on it, picking it up gently. The pup bit Adrian hard on the hand. "Good boy! You should bite me, at least for now. Good spirit, and you're obviously loyal to a fault. You're going home with me. Maybe I'll call you bear, just to confuse people."

Adrian rode carrying the pup. After a few days' of being held and hand fed, it quit trying to bite him. After two weeks it accepted Adrian as friendly and didn't try to escape, instead following him closely as he attended to camp chores. Adrian fed the pup jerky and pemmican at regular intervals. It quickly regained its health. He had become a good companion.

He arrived in the village with the crushing sense of foreboding that had been gnawing at his gut for the three weeks the trip had taken. Roman had called him home saying they were facing a disaster, an event that could mean the death of every man, woman, and child in the village. But Roman wouldn't say more than that on the radio. Adrian had to live with the open ended statement until he returned home. It had created such a sense of urgency that he pushed his horse to near death to get home as fast as he could.

Roman gave Adrian a hard hug. "Glad you made it back safely, we've got big trouble coming and need your help bad."

"Tell me about it."

THE END

Made in the USA
Lexington, KY
07 June 2013